I0637746

# Where There's Smoke: A Texas Love Story

## A Texas Love Story, Volume 1

### Rees Walther

Published by Rees Walther, 2025.

ISBN 979-8-9928392-1-0 Paperback
ISBN 979-8-9928392-2-7 Ebook
Published by
Rocket Smoked Publishing
Second edition 2026

# Dedication

To my mother, whose love, wisdom, and unwavering belief in me still guide my steps. Your absence is felt in every moment, yet your presence remains in all that I do. You instilled in me a deep sense of creativity and a love for life that continues to shape my journey. This book is a tribute to the strength, imagination, and joy you nurtured in me.

And to my wife, my rock, my pillar of strength—your love and support are the foundation upon which I build my dreams. Thank you for standing beside me through every challenge and every triumph.

This book is for both of you.

# Chapter 1

# A Call from Home

Mae Whitaker had always thought of New York City as the place where dreams come true. For ten years, it had been her playground, her proving ground, and her sanctuary. The city's pulse matched her own—fast, driven, relentless. Every morning, she walked with purpose down Fifth Avenue, her polished heels clicking in time with the city's unrelenting rhythm. The deep green leather tote on her shoulder was a staple, a silent nod to control. To belonging. To success. She fit seamlessly into the city's landscape—polished, put-together, yet always in motion.

The city was its own symphony. Car horns blared impatiently, taxis skidded to abrupt halts, and pedestrians wove through the sidewalks like a perfectly rehearsed dance. Street vendors called out their breakfast specials, the scent of warm bagels and crisp bacon mingling with the cool bite of the lingering March air. The mirrored facades of towering buildings reflected the hurried strides of men and women in tailored suits, their coffee cups an extension of their hands. The rhythm of it all made Mae feel alive—unstoppable.

The sleek, glass-walled coffee shop on the ground floor of her office building was a familiar refuge, a microcosm of the city itself. Floor-to-ceiling windows welcomed the golden slant of morning light, bouncing off polished oak counters and gleaming brass espresso machines. Dark green leather banquettes lined the far wall, softened by years of loyal patrons. Pendant lights, encased in smoked glass, cast a warm, amber glow over the space. The air was thick with the intoxicating aroma of freshly ground Ethiopian and Guatemalan beans, caramelized sugar, and buttery croissants warming behind the glass pastry case. Hints of cinnamon and vanilla lingered, weaving through the murmurs of early risers. The low hum of indie music barely registered against the rhythm of morning—hissing steam wands, the rhythmic tap of a barista tamping espresso, bursts of laughter punctuating the air.

Mae stepped inside, the warmth wrapping around her like a well-worn embrace. The contrast was instant—outside, the city was crisp and unrelenting; inside, it was a haven of roasted coffee and indulgence.

"Morning, Mae! Let me guess—large caramel macchiato, extra caramel drizzle?" The voice, smooth and teasing, belonged to Adam—the barista who had somehow memorized her order from her very first visit.

"You know me too well, Adam." Mae smiled, pulling her wallet from her tote.

Adam flashed a knowing grin, already reaching for a ceramic cup. He moved with effortless ease, his auburn curls slightly tousled, the faintest shadow of stubble lining his jaw. The sleeves of his fitted black t-shirt were pushed up, revealing intricate tattoos—constellations, delicate floral designs, and a cursive phrase that Mae had never quite managed to decipher. A silver hoop gleamed in his nose as he turned, his forest-green eyes crinkling at the edges as he expertly worked the espresso machine.

"You always say 'extra caramel,' but I'm pretty sure you mean 'just a cup of caramel with a splash of coffee,'" Adam teased, setting the drink in front of her with a flourish.

Mae laughed, her fingers brushing his as she reached for the cup. The warmth seeped into her hands, smooth and indulgent, the perfect balance of sweetness and strength.

Just then, a familiar tune started playing from the overhead speakers. *Blue Skies* by Willie Nelson. The soft, twangy chords drifted through the café, weaving between the hum of espresso machines and the low murmur of early morning conversations. Mae frowned, half-listening as Willie's easy, unhurried voice filled the space. The song felt out of place here, buried beneath the city's constant thrum, like a postcard from a past she had left behind.

She stirred her coffee, trying to ignore the unexpected pull of nostalgia. Texas, home, had a way of sneaking up on her when she least expected it.

Behind her, the rhythmic clicking of heels signaled the arrival of Jenny Torres. Mae didn't have to turn around to know it was her best friend—the sound was unmistakable, sharp and confident, like the woman herself.

"Dios mío, you're such a creature of habit. Coffee, work, sleep, repeat. When's the last time you did something unexpected?" Jenny teased, her voice tinged with the warm cadence of her Puerto Rican heritage. Her accent curled around her words in the way Mae had always envied—effortless, melodic, steeped in home.

Jenny had a way of commanding attention, whether she meant to or not. Today, she wore a fitted navy blazer, cinched at the waist over a crisp white blouse, paired with high-waisted charcoal trousers that elongated her already statuesque frame. Gold hoop earrings—the kind her mother had given her at her quinceañera—peeked through the cascade of glossy dark curls tumbling down her back. She smelled of jasmine and citrus, a perfume passed down through generations.

Mae took a slow sip of her coffee, savoring the caramel as Jenny gave her an appraising look.

"Jenny, life is too short for bitter coffee," Mae said, playful. "Besides, isn't that what caffeine is for? To make life a little sweeter?"

Jenny rolled her eyes, flipping a curl over her shoulder. "I'd argue that's what dating is for." She arched an eyebrow. "Speaking of, when was the last time you actually went on a date?"

Mae groaned, stirring her coffee unnecessarily. "Don't start."

The coffee shop hummed around them. Near the window, a man in a navy suit sat hunched over his laptop, fingers flying over the keyboard between sips of black coffee. Across from him, a woman in a sleek trench coat scrolled through her phone, her untouched latte cooling by the second. In the corner, a group of students debated over open textbooks, their voices rising and falling in tandem with the city outside.

Jenny leaned against the counter, tapping her manicured nails against the surface. "Come on, Mae," she pressed. "You work too hard. When's the last time you let loose?"

Mae sighed, feigning deep contemplation. "Well, I did order an extra caramel drizzle today."

Jenny groaned, throwing her hands up. "Ay, por favor! That doesn't count!" She gestured wildly, nearly knocking into a passing customer, who chuckled in amusement. "You need something exciting, something different. Let me set you up with someone."

Mae narrowed her eyes. "I don't know, Jenny. The last time you set me up, the guy talked about his stock portfolio the entire night."

Jenny placed a hand over her heart. "Okay, that was a mistake. But this time, I promise—someone fun, someone spontaneous."

Adam, listening with quiet amusement, slid another cup onto the counter. "Jenny, your double espresso is ready. No sugar, just like your dating standards."

Jenny shot him a withering look before cracking a grin. "You're lucky you make good coffee, Adam."

As Mae took her cup, a slow smile curved her lips. The coffee shop wasn't just part of her morning routine; it was an anchor, a pocket of familiarity in a city that never stopped moving. Friendships thrived here, woven into the fabric of warm espresso and easy banter. No matter how chaotic the world outside became, there was always a steady hum of conversation, the hiss of steaming milk, and a perfectly crafted cup waiting for her inside.

Mae groaned, nudging Jenny lightly with her elbow, the rich scent of caramel and espresso curling between them like an embrace. "Don't start. I've been busy. You know, climbing the corporate ladder and all that."

Jenny snorted, shaking her head as her gold hoop earrings glinted under the café's amber lighting. "Oh, please. Even CEOs date. Come on, Mae, you're smart, gorgeous, and honestly, a little intimidating. You can't tell me no one's interested."

Mae smirked, bringing her cup to her glossy red lips. The warmth seeped into her fingers, the caramel drizzle pooling like liquid gold atop the frothy milk. She took a slow sip, savoring the contrast between the bold espresso and its velvety sweetness before finally answering. "Oh, they're interested," she said, setting her cup down with a soft clink. "But interested doesn't mean much when all they want is someone to look good on their arm at corporate parties. My job doesn't exactly scream 'home by six to cook dinner.'"

Jenny let out a sharp laugh, loud enough to turn a few heads. "And thank God for that. Who wants to be arm candy anyway?" She tucked a curl behind her ear and leaned forward, lowering her voice to a conspiratorial whisper. "But seriously, what ever happened to that Wall Street guy? The one you were seeing a few weeks ago? You actually sounded excited about him."

Mae stirred her coffee absentmindedly, watching the caramel swirl through the foam. "Oh, you mean Mr. 'Let's Get Married' after the third date?"

Jenny nearly choked on her espresso, setting her cup down with a clatter. "No way! He actually brought up marriage that soon?"

"Not just mentioned it," Mae said, rolling her eyes. "He had a whole plan. House in the Hamptons, three kids, golden retriever—he even talked about what kind of joint credit card we should get."

Jenny grimaced. "Yikes. Okay, fair. But at least he wasn't married."

Mae arched a brow, smirking. "Unlike your last boyfriend? The one you dated for six months?"

Jenny groaned dramatically, placing a hand over her heart. "Ugh, don't remind me. I swear, I didn't know. If I had, do you really think I would've wasted half a year of my life?"

"Only you, Jenny," Mae teased, shaking her head, affection laced through her voice. "What's your track record now? Three cheaters and a guy who ghosted you on Valentine's Day?"

Jenny shrugged, unbothered. "Hey, at least my love life is entertaining. Besides, you're one to talk. When's the last time you let loose? I'm talking about the old Mae—the one who danced on tables in college and dared frat boys to chug tequila."

Mae laughed, warmth creeping into her chest. "You mean the Mae who ended up puking in your dorm room trash can while you lectured me about hydration?"

"Exactly," Jenny said with a grin. "God, remember that night? That frat guy you dared tried to impress us by downing two shots at once and passed out cold. We thought he'd died."

"And you called campus security!" Mae added, doubling over in laughter. "They showed up, saw him drooling on the couch, and just rolled their eyes."

"Good times," Jenny said wistfully. "Back when life was simple, and the biggest decision we had to make was where to order pizza from."

Mae shook her head, still smiling. "Yeah. And now here we are, trading frat parties for morning coffee runs and talking about exes who should've stayed in therapy."

The coffee shop buzzed louder as the morning rush reached its peak. Jenny glanced around, frowning. "This chaos gives me anxiety. How do you find comfort in it?"

Mae shrugged, cradling her coffee. "It's predictable. I know what to expect every morning. The same coffee, the same faces, the same routine." Her gaze lingered on the clean lines of the café's modern decor, the subtle symmetry of it all. "I like order, cleanliness, regularity..." She trailed off, her expression thoughtful. "Even the architecture here makes sense. Nothing out of place. It's the opposite of how I grew up."

Jenny's brows lifted. "You mean in Texas?"

"Yeah," Mae said, her voice softening. "Everything there runs on a different kind of time. Slower. My dad used to drive the speed limit on those endless West Texas highways, pulling over if someone came up behind him going even a little faster. He'd say, 'No need to rush, Mae. Life'll wait for you.'"

Jenny's eyes widened. "You're kidding."

"I wish I were," Mae said, chuckling. "But that's just how it was. Slow, steady, predictable. And I couldn't wait to get out of there."

Jenny leaned closer, searching Mae's face. "And now you've convinced yourself you like the exact opposite. But do you really? Or is it just what you've gotten used to?"

Mae hesitated, her fingers tightening around her cup. "I don't know," she admitted. "Maybe both."

Mae shifted the conversation before her intro-spection could spiral. "How do you even juggle it all? You're a paralegal by day and a chaos magnet by night."

Jenny shrugged, flashing a knowing grin. "It's all about balance, my friend. Unlike you, Miss Workaholic, I actually take vacations. Puerto Rico every year, like clockwork. If I skipped even once, my mom and abuela would be on the next flight up here, dragging me to the airport by my hair and personally ensuring I never missed another."

Mae snorted. "Must be nice to have a built-in vacation enforcer."

Jenny's laughter softened, and a knowing look settled into her dark eyes. "You know, Mae, you could use a trip home. When's the last time you visited Texas?"

Mae hesitated, her fingers tightening around her cup. "Three years ago. Christmas. I was supposed to stay two weeks, but my boss called me back early. I left the day after Christmas."

Jenny blinked, incredulous. "Three years? Mae, come on. Don't you miss your family?"

"Of course I do," Mae said, her voice quieter now. "It's just... hard to find the time. And honestly? I've convinced myself I prefer it here. The chaos mixed with the structure. The order."

Jenny leaned in, resting her forearms on the table. "Mae, if you keep waiting for the perfect time to visit, it'll never come. And when something happens, you'll wish you'd gone sooner."

Before Mae could answer, a sharp vibration against the wooden table cut through their conversation. Her phone. The screen lit up with a single word: **Dad.**

Her breath hitched. Her father never called during the day. Not on a Wednesday morning. The only other time he had done that was five years ago—when her grandfather passed away.

Jenny noticed the shift in Mae's expression immediately. Her teasing demeanor fell away as she leaned in slightly. "What is it?"

Mae swallowed hard, her pulse quickening. "It's my dad." She didn't realize how tight she was gripping her cup until she forced her fingers to unclench. "He never calls during the day."

"Maybe it's a butt dial," Jenny offered, though her voice carried more hope than certainty.

Mae exhaled slowly and gently picked up her coffee cup. Finding a quieter spot near the door, she took a steadying breath, bracing herself before pressing the phone to her ear.

"Dad?" she said, her voice tight with unspoken worry.

# Chapter 2

# Dad's Call

H er father's voice came through the line, low and heavy. "Mae... it's your mom. She... she's not doing well. The doctor says... well, you should come home. Now."

The world around her faded. The bustling hum of the café, the aroma of espresso, the clatter of cups—it all turned into a distant blur, like a radio station losing signal. Her fingers went numb, her grip loosening until her coffee nearly slipped from her grasp.

"What?" Her own voice sounded foreign, thin. "What do you mean? What's wrong with her?"

She pressed the phone harder to her ear, as if that would change his response. The silence stretched too long before her father's voice came again, low and unsteady.

"It's her heart, Mae. The doctors think it's gotten worse," he said, his voice cracking. The raw emotion in his words was unlike anything Mae had ever heard from him—a man who had always prided himself on being steady, unshakable. "We're at the hospital. They're running tests, but... the doctor thinks it's serious."

Mae's breath hitched, a sharp pang slicing through her chest. "But... she's been on medication. The last time I talked to her, she said the doctors were managing it."

"I know, sweetheart," he said, his voice heavy with exhaustion. "We all thought it was under control. But something's changed."

Her mother had always been the strongest person she knew—the one who made Sunday breakfasts feel like a sacred ritual, the one who laughed the loudest at her own jokes, the one who smelled like cinnamon and home. The idea of her being weak, vulnerable, lying in a hospital bed—it didn't fit. It couldn't.

Her hands trembled as she tried to form words, but none came. The floor felt unsteady beneath her, the weight of the news pressing down with suffocating force. A barista called out an order somewhere in the background, a jarring contrast to the storm roaring inside her.

"Okay," she finally managed, her voice barely above a whisper. "I'll book a flight tonight."

"Thank you, sweetheart." Her father's voice wavered, betraying the emotion he rarely let surface. "She'll want to see you."

But Mae could hear what he wasn't saying. **I need you here too.**

She swallowed against the lump forming in her throat. "I'll be there soon."

As the call ended, Mae stared blankly at her phone, her mind struggling to catch up with reality. As she lowered her phone with trembling fingers, the café noise slowly crept back into focus, but she felt detached, as if watching everything through a pane of glass. Her world had just shifted, and yet, for everyone else, life continued unchanged.

Her father had always been the rock of their family—calm, composed, a man of few words but unwavering devotion.

He wasn't just her dad—he was Mr. Whitaker to generations of Twinsdale students, the kind of high school history teacher who made dusty textbooks come alive with stories and debates. And to Mae, he was Coach Dad too—whistle around his neck at basketball practice, standing on the sidelines during Friday night football games, always there, steady as the scoreboard.

And yet, in that moment, Mae heard the heartbreak in his voice, the helplessness he rarely showed. He had loved her mother for forty-five years, their marriage a quiet testament to enduring love. If he was shaken, it meant things were bad. Worse than she wanted to believe.

She took a breath, forcing her feet to move, heading back toward the table where Jenny was waiting. Each step felt heavier than the last, as if the gravity of the moment was pulling her down. Her fingers curled around her phone, white-knuckled, her expression unreadable—somewhere between shock and deep thought.

The memories of home collided with the stark reality of a hospital room, beeping monitors, and uncertainty. Her mother's laughter echoed in her mind, blending with the scent of cinnamon and vanilla from their Sunday baking sessions. But all of that felt so distant now, replaced by the fear that she might lose the person who had always been her soft place to land.

By the time she reached the table, Jenny was already leaning forward, concern etched into her features. "Mae?"

Mae sank into her chair, her posture stiff, her eyes fixed on the coffee cup in front of her. The warmth of the ceramic felt distant against her fingers, as if she were holding onto something slipping away.

"Mae?" Jenny's voice softened. "What is it? What happened?"

"It's... my mom." The words felt foreign, unreal. "She's in the hospital. Dad says... it's serious."

Jenny's expression shifted, her teasing demeanor gone. "Oh, Mae. I'm so sorry." She reached across the table, her hand resting firmly over Mae's. "What can I do? Do you need help booking a flight? Calling your boss?"

Mae swallowed hard, her mind spiraling through all the logistics she had to manage. **Twinsdale, Texas.** A place she hadn't been in over three years, now pulling her back like an unbreakable thread. And this time, there was no choice.

She shook her head, blinking back the stinging in her eyes. "I just... I don't even know where to start."

"It's okay," Jenny said, her voice steady. "Start by breathing. One thing at a time. We'll figure this out together."

Mae nodded, inhaling shakily. "I have vacation days. I never use them. But my boss—" She exhaled sharply, frustration and fear battling in her chest. "He doesn't like when people take time off. It's an unspoken rule at my firm."

Jenny's eyes darkened. "Mae, this is your **mom.** Your boss can shove his unspoken rules where the sun doesn't shine."

Mae let out a weak laugh, though the weight of the moment crushed any humor. "I know. I just... I'm up for a promotion. Executive Vice President. If I leave now, what if—"

Jenny cut her off, her voice firm. "Mae. Your mom is more important than any promotion. You're brilliant at what you do, and if your boss doesn't see that, he doesn't deserve you. Call him. Lay it out. You have to go home."

Mae nodded, her resolve hardening. She pulled out her phone and dialed her boss. The conversation was exactly as she expected—tense.

"Look, Mae, I understand that this is a personal emergency, but we have a lot riding on this project," Marc said, his voice clipped. "You're up for a major promotion. Your presence right now is critical."

She clenched her jaw. "I know. And I'm committed to my work. But my mother is in the hospital. I need to be there."

There was a pause—just long enough to be calculated. "We can delay your deadline by a week, but I need you back within two. The executive board needs to see consistency."

Her stomach knotted. "Consistency? Marc, I've worked overtime for months. I haven't taken a single personal day in over a year."

Another pause. "I know. Which is why I'm trying to help you, Mae. But I have to consider the team. If you're unavailable, we may need to look at alternative leader-ship. There are others who are eager to step up."

And there it was—the unspoken threat. The promotion, the career she had built from the ground up, dangled in front of her like a prize she could lose if she didn't comply.

Mae forced her voice to remain steady. "I'll be back as soon as I can."

"That's all I ask," Marc said smoothly, as if the conversation had been entirely reasonable. "Take care of your family. We'll hold things together—for now."

She ended the call, gripping her phone so tightly her knuckles turned white. The walls of the café felt suddenly smaller, closing in. How had she given so much to this company, only to be treated as replaceable the moment she needed something in return?

Jenny's voice cut through her spiraling thoughts. "Mae? What happened?"

Mae exhaled sharply. "Nothing unexpected. I need to go home and start packing," Mae said, slipping her phone into her pocket, already cataloging the things she needed to do.

Jenny studied her face for a long moment before nodding. "Yeah, I have to head into work for a few hours, but as soon as I'm done, I'll come over to help you get ready." She gave Mae's arm a reassuring squeeze. "You don't have to do this alone. We'll get through it."

Mae managed a small, grateful smile. "Thanks, Jen."

They parted ways, and Mae stepped onto the bustling sidewalk. The usual comfort of the city's rhythm—the constant movement, the predictability—felt different now. Hollow. Distant. She barely registered the walk home, her thoughts a tangled mess of memories, worry, and the suffocating uncertainty of what awaited her in Texas.

By the time she unlocked her apartment door, exhaustion had already settled deep in her bones. And she hadn't even left yet.

The doorbell rang, and Mae hurried to answer it. She pulled the door open to reveal Jenny, who took one look at her and stepped inside without hesitation.

"Hey," Jenny said, her voice warm with concern. "How are you holding up?"

Mae let out a tired sigh, her shoulders slumping. "I don't know. It feels surreal. I know I have to go, but I just..." She trailed off, shaking her head as if trying to make sense of the emotions tangled inside her.

Jenny squeezed her arm gently. "You don't have to know. You just have to take it one step at a time."

Stepping further inside, Jenny stopped abruptly, eyes widening as she took in the state of Mae's apartment. Suitcases lay half-packed on the bed, clothes were strewn across the floor, and a pair of heels sat abandoned in the middle of the rug like a forgotten afterthought. Normally, Mae's space was a reflection of her—sleek, modern, impossibly put-together. Now, it looked as if a hurricane had swept through it. The stainless steel appliances in the open kitchen gleamed under the soft glow of pendant lighting, contrasting sharply with the chaos surrounding them.

"Mae," Jenny said, lifting an eyebrow. "What happened in here?"

Mae groaned, running a hand through her hair. "Packing happened. And apparently, I suck at it."

Jenny smirked. "It looks more like unpacking."

Mae sighed dramatically, holding up a pair of jeans in defeat. "I don't even own Texas clothes anymore." She gestured at the pile beside her. "I have one pair of jeans, a Longhorns sweatshirt, and maybe four t-shirts. What do people even wear in Twinsdale these days?"

Jenny snorted. "I'm pretty sure jeans and t-shirts are still acceptable. Relax, you're not walking into a fashion show."

Mae shot her a withering look. "And how many pairs of underwear am I supposed to pack? What if I stay longer than two weeks? Do I bring dress clothes in case I need to hop on a work call?" Her voice was rising, her frustration slipping through the cracks.

Jenny held up a hand, her tone soothing. "Mae. Breathe. You're panicking about packing because you're panicking about your mom. It's okay. Just pack what you have. If you need more, you can always buy it there. Twinsdale does have stores, right?"

Mae exhaled, her shoulders dropping slightly. "You're right. I just... I don't know how to do this. How to go back. What if—"

Jenny cut her off gently, not letting her finish the thought. "You don't have to have it all figured out. You just have to show up. That's what matters."

Mae let out a slow breath, nodding. "You're right. But there's still so much to figure out." She rubbed her temples, her voice rising as she spoke faster. "Okay, so I booked a flight—earliest one I could get—it's a 6am departure to Dallas, not Austin, because guess what? The only flight into Austin doesn't get there until tomorrow night! Tomorrow night, Jenny! That's not even an option."

Jenny opened her mouth to say something, but Mae kept going, the frustration pouring out. "And then I realized—great, I land in Dallas, but I can't ask Dad to pick me up. He needs to be with Mom, not spending six hours driving back and forth just to get me. So I thought, okay, rental car. Easy, right? Wrong. No rental drop-offs in Twinsdale! Because why would that be convenient? So now I'm looking at a three-hour drive, early in the morning, after barely sleeping on the plane."

Jenny gave her a sympathetic look. "Mae, breathe."

Mae let out a sharp exhale, pressing her fingers to her forehead. "I know, I know. I just—every single thing is harder than it needs to be. And I just want to be there already."

Jenny rested a reassuring hand on Mae's arm. "I get it. We'll figure it out. But you're going to get there, okay? That's what matters."

Mae nodded, forcing herself to inhale slowly. "Okay. Yeah. You're right. I just... need to keep moving."

She threw her hands up, exasperated, then let them fall to her sides. "So, I rented the car for two weeks. Because that seemed reasonable. Two weeks, right? That's what I told my boss. That's what I'm telling myself. So I should be back in two weeks, right?" She let out a dry laugh, shaking her head. "But what if I'm not? What if I have to extend it?"

Jenny gave her a look but didn't press. Instead, she watched as Mae zipped up her suitcase, her expression turning thoughtful. "Why haven't you gone back more often?" she finally asked, her voice gentle, not accusatory.

Mae hesitated, feeling the weight of the question settle over her. Twinsdale wasn't just a place—it was a time capsule of memories, emotions, and choices she had spent years locking away. She had built a life in New York, one that was structured, ambitious, relentless. But going back meant confronting everything she had left behind.

"I guess... I've just been so focused on proving myself. Proving that I could make it on my own," she admitted, her voice barely above a whisper. "Every promotion, every late night, every sacrifice—it was all about moving forward. And every time I thought about going back, it felt like admitting I needed something outside of myself. Like I wasn't strong enough to do it all on my own."

Jenny raised an eyebrow. "Mae, you're thriving in New York. Going home doesn't erase that."

"I know," Mae said quietly. "But it's not just that. It's the pace. New York keeps me moving, always pushing forward. Another project, another goal, another reason to keep running. Going home... it forces me to stop. And I don't know if I can handle that." She swallowed hard, her gaze drifting. "Because when I slow down, I start thinking. About the choices I made. About what I left behind."

Jenny stepped closer, her voice soft but firm. "Mae, no one's keeping score except you. You're allowed to go home. And you're allowed to be scared. You're allowed to slow down."

Mae nodded, blinking back the sting of tears. Jenny's words settled deep, shaking something loose inside her. She had spent so long building walls around herself, mistaking movement for progress, thinking if she just kept running, she could somehow prove herself worthy. She didn't know to whom, maybe just to herself.

# Chapter 3

# The Trip Home

The next morning, as Mae stood near the terminal window waiting to board, she pressed her forehead against the cool glass and looked out at the runway. Beyond the scattered lights of taxiing planes, the New York City skyline stretched across the horizon, bathed in the hushed glow of dawn. The city she had claimed as her own. The city she had fought to belong to. And yet, as she stood there, watching it from a distance, she realized something unsettling—it had never really felt like home.

She clutched the strap of her bag as she moved down the jet bridge, her steps slower than usual. The weight of exhaustion clung to her shoulders, but it wasn't just from the lack of sleep. It was from the last few years, from the way she had poured everything into building a life here—one that, at this moment, felt strangely hollow.

Her mother's voice echoed in her mind, warm and teasing. *Don't work yourself into the ground, baby. Life is more than just the next goalpost.* Mae had always smiled and waved it off, convinced that ambition was the tradeoff for happiness. And yet, standing in a crowded airport, surrounded by hundreds of strangers moving in every direction, she had never felt so alone.

New York was supposed to be a place of reinvention, of possibility. And in many ways, it had been. She had the job, the apartment with the overpriced view, the routine of caramel macchiatos and late-night takeout. But what did she really have beyond that?

Jenny was the only person who truly knew her here. Adam, her barista, was friendly in that easy, uncommitted way that made her morning coffee runs feel less isolating. Her coworkers? They were pleasant but distant, always too busy rushing from one meeting to the next to form anything resembling real friendship. The city was always moving, people brushing past her in hurried strides, barely looking up.

There was something painfully ironic about feeling lonely in a city of eight million people.

She swallowed against the lump in her throat as she found her seat and sank into it. The hum of the engines vibrated beneath her feet, grounding her in the present moment. Soon, she'd be thousands of miles away, back in the town she had once tried to escape. A town where people waved when they passed each other on the street, where grocery store clerks remembered your name, where the air smelled of fresh-cut grass and sweet tea in the summer.

The thought of her father, of his quiet strength and the way he carried the weight of everything without complaint, sent a pang through her chest. He needed her. Her mother needed her.

But was she ready to be there again?

The pilot's voice crackled through the speaker, announcing their departure. Mae gripped the armrest as the plane began to taxi. Outside her window, the New York skyline stretched across the horizon, bathed in the hushed glow of dawn. The jagged silhouettes of skyscrapers pierced the soft lavender sky, their glass facades catching the first hints of gold from the rising sun. The Empire State Building stood resolute, its beacon blinking against the fading darkness, while the bridges arched over the Hudson, their lights flickering like distant constellations. The streets, once relentless with their honking and hurried footsteps, were momentarily subdued, as if the city itself had paused to take a breath before the inevitable chaos of the day.

Mae exhaled, her breath fogging the glass. It was beautiful—everything she had worked for, everything she had built. And yet, as she watched the city shrink beneath the plane's ascent, a strange hollowness settled within her that she couldn't explain.

Mae closed her eyes, and for a moment, she was twenty-two again, standing in the lobby of a sleek, glass-paneled high-rise in Midtown. Her heels clicked against the marble floor as she approached the receptionist, her stomach twisting with nerves and exhilaration. It was her first day as a junior associate at one of the most sought-after firms in the city—a job she had clawed her way into with relentless ambition and a résumé packed with internships, late nights, and sheer determination.

She had made it.

When she stepped into her cubicle for the first time, the scent of fresh paper and burnt espresso filled the air. She ran her fingers over the crisp, white business card sitting neatly on her desk—her name embossed in bold lettering, the company's logo gleaming in silver foil. This was it. The moment she had spent years working toward.

That night, she celebrated with Jenny, who had a similar experience the year before, on the rooftop of a tiny bar in the East Village. The city stretched out before them, endless and alive, neon lights bouncing off rain-slicked streets.

"Here's to proving them all wrong," Jenny had said, raising her glass with a smirk.

Mae had laughed, clinking her drink against Jenny's. "Here's to never going back."

She had meant it. Back then, Twinsdale had felt like a life half-lived—a place where people stayed, married their high school sweethearts, and spent Sundays at the same diner, ordering the same breakfast they had eaten since childhood. She had wanted more. She had wanted the challenge, the rush, the unpredictability of a city that never slept.

But now, as the plane climbed higher and higher, that version of herself felt like a stranger. Was it ambition that had driven her? Or just fear of being trapped in a place she never truly gave a chance?

She exhaled, opening her eyes. Below, the last edges of the skyline disappeared beneath a layer of clouds. The life she had built—the one she had been so desperate for—was slipping further away.

Home was three hours past Dallas, in a town where the stars stretched wide and clear, where time moved slower, where the people she loved most were waiting for her.

She tightened her grip on the armrest as the plane ascended, her heart heavy with uncertainty. This wasn't just a trip. It was a reckoning—with her past, her choices, and the life she had built. And as much as she feared what lay ahead, she knew one thing for certain: it was time to go home.

The plane touched down with a jarring thud, the tires screeching against the tarmac before settling into a steady roll. As Mae stepped off the jet bridge and into the terminal, the shift was immediate. The familiarity of men in cowboy boots, women in beaded jeans and Texas flags strewn on every item imaginable at each gift store.

Outside, the air was different too—thicker, warmer, carrying the faint scent of a light rain on sunbaked asphalt and wild sage instead of hot dog stands and taxi exhaust. She pulled off her blazer and stuffed it into her carry-on, suddenly feeling overdressed among the laid-back airport crowd.

The rental car lot was nearly empty, the attendant giving her a lazy nod as she slid into the driver's seat of a silver SUV. She adjusted the mirrors, gripping the unfamiliar wheel, and for a long moment, she just sat there.

This was real now.

With a deep breath, she pulled out onto the freeway, leaving the city behind. The skyline of Dallas disappeared in the rearview mirror, replaced by open land stretching for miles, the sky wider than she remembered. Gone were the towering glass buildings, the flashing bill-boards, the tightly packed streets. Out here, everything had room to breathe.

Mae merged off the freeway onto the winding highway leading to Twinsdale, the Texas landscape unfurling before her in endless stretches of open fields, wide skies, and the faint rise of hills in the distance. It had been years since she'd seen this view, and after so much time surrounded by skyscrapers and hurried streets, the vastness of it all felt jarring—yet so familiar, like a song she hadn't heard in years but still knew by heart.

Along the roadside, clusters of bluebonnets stretched toward the horizon, their deep indigo petals swaying gently in the early spring breeze. The sight of them tugged at something deep within her, a reminder of childhood drives along these same roads, of her mother pointing them out through the window and insisting they stop for pictures. March had always been a time of renewal here, when the earth shook off winter's last chill and burst into color, a quiet kind of magic unique to Texas.

Her phone buzzed, and her father's name lit up the screen. She pressed the button on the car's hands-free system, steadying her breath before answering.

"Hey, Dad." She kept her voice even, though the nerves inside her churned like a storm cloud ready to break.

"Hey, sweetheart." His voice was warm but edged with fatigue, the weight of the past few days bleeding through. "We're heading home from the hospital now. The doctors have done all they can for now. They've run every test they needed."

Mae's grip tightened on the steering wheel, her knuckles paling. "And… what happens next?" she asked carefully. She knew her father too well—he had a way of skimming over details, of shielding her from the full gravity of things until he was sure she could handle it.

There was a pause, and she could almost hear the way he pressed his lips together, debating how much to say. "They're setting her up with monitoring equipment at home. Doctor Abbott will stop by later tonight to check on her, and…" He hesitated, and Mae braced herself. "He should have some of the test results by then."

Mae swallowed, the weight of unspoken fears settling in her thoughts. Pushing him for more wouldn't change anything, and right now, she wasn't sure she wanted to hear the words out loud. "Okay," she said softly. "I'll be there soon. Probably another two hours."

Her father exhaled, a sound heavy with emotions he wouldn't voice. "Drive safe. And remember—this is West Texas, not back East. No weaving through traffic like you're still in New York." There was a slight crack in his voice before he cleared his throat. "Your mom's going to be so happy to see you."

Mae blinked against the sting behind her eyes. "Me too, Dad. Me too."

As the call ended, silence settled back into the car, other than the hum of the tires on the pavement and the rhythmic whisper of the wind rushing past. She let her gaze flicker between the open road and the horizon stretching infinitely ahead. Each mile carried her farther from the life she had built and closer to the one she had left behind. The towering buildings, the flashing neon lights, the city that had consumed her every waking hour—those things felt distant now, like echoes of another version of herself.

With every passing minute, home wasn't just a place she was returning to; it was something that was pulling her back, piece by piece.

# Chapter 4

# Homecoming

Mae eased off the gas as she rolled into town, the speed limit dropping to twenty-five miles per hour. Not that she needed a sign to remind her—driving slow was just how things were done here. But there it was anyway, standing tall at the town's entrance: **"Our town is like Heaven to us. Please don't drive like Hell through it."**

She let out a breath of amusement, the familiar words reminding her of days gone by. That sign had been there for as long as she could remember, a small-town warning wrapped in charm. How many times had she passed it without thinking twice? Now, after years of city life where honking and lane-cutting were as common as breathing, it felt almost like a challenge to slow down—to really be here.

The first thing she saw was the old Chevron station, standing like a weary sentry at the town's edge. It had once been a hub of small-town life, where neighbors caught up as their tanks filled, where her grandfather worked with the quiet ease of someone who loved what he did.

Now, it looked drained of life. The once-bright sign drooped, its colors dulled by sun and neglect, and the gas pumps stood motionless, their hoses curled like abandoned garden snakes. The service bay doors—once always open, revealing her grandfather wiping grease from his hands with a well-worn rag—were locked shut. In her mind, she could still hear the cheerful ding-ding of the service bell, but it was nothing more than an echo now. The out-of-towner who had bought it after her grandfather passed clearly didn't care for it the same way. The cracked pavement, the dirty windows, the missing letters on the sign—it all spoke of something Mae wasn't ready to name.

A hundred feet ahead, Peterson's Market stood just where it always had, tucked neatly into the second block of Main Street. The store had been there as long as the town itself, and despite the peeling paint on the wooden sign and the way the awning sagged slightly on one side, it still had the same quiet charm. Inside, Mae knew the floors were the same scuffed linoleum she'd walked across as a child, and the scent of fresh produce mixed with something old and familiar, like time settling in its place.

She imagined Mrs. Peterson behind the register, peering over her reading glasses as she rang up a sale, nodding to customers she'd known since they were kids. This was the kind of store where people still scribbled grocery tabs in a well-worn notebook, where a ten-year-old could ride their bike up, grab a cold soda, and promise to pay next time without question. Mae smiled slightly, comforted by its persistence. Some places didn't change because they didn't need to.

The post office came next, its squat brick building standing proudly against the sky, its white trim chipped but enduring. The stone steps leading to the entrance were worn smooth by decades of footfalls, a silent testament to the stories that had passed through its doors. This was more than a place for letters—it was the town's unofficial information hub. Mae noticed the cluster of older women gathered near the front, their voices rising and falling as they exchanged the latest town news. She had no doubt that her mother's health had been a frequent subject today, passed along in hushed tones and scattered like letters—sealed, delivered, and spread across town.

Just ahead, at the start of the final block, Sally's Sweets Shop came into view, its cheerful pink sign still standing out against the weathered storefronts around it. The glass display window was covered in its signature pastel swirls, advertising homemade fudge, fresh-baked pies, and hand-dipped ice cream. It had always been a happy place, a bright spot in town, and just seeing it made Mae's heart lift a little.

She could still remember walking in after school, the bell over the door jingling as she followed her mother inside, eager for a scoop of vanilla bean while her mom picked out pecan pralines. The scent of sugar and butter still seemed to linger in the air, and Mae had no doubt that if she stepped inside, she'd find the same glass jars of old-fashioned candy lined up on the counter, waiting for a new generation of kids to press their noses against the glass.

Directly across the street, Rocket Ribs and BBQ stood in bold contrast, its red and black sign a sharp statement against the muted tones of the other shops.

The scent of slow-smoked meat drifted across the road, wrapping around Sally's Sweets like a perfect pairing of salt and sugar.

Mae smiled to herself. *Rocket.* The nickname had started back in high school, when her dad—Coach Whitaker—had watched a scrawny sophomore named Jim Carter hurl a perfect spiral down the field and muttered, "That kid can throw a football like a rocket." The name stuck. And now, all these years later, the monicker had become more than a nickname. It was a business. A brand.

The restaurant occupied what was once the old farmers' co-op, a building that had sat vacant for years before being reborn into something new. The structure itself was still sturdy, its broad frame a reminder of its past, but the transformation was unmistakable. Where cattle troughs and tractors for sale had once lined the front, there was now a sprawling outdoor porch that wrapped around to the side, complete with wooden picnic tables and strings of soft, glowing lights that would flicker to life in the evening. At the far end of the porch sat the heart of the operation—a massive smoker made from an old propane tank, its blackened steel giving away just how many years it had spent cooking meat to perfection.

It was newer—at least by this town's standards—but it had already cemented itself as a Main Street staple. A place where regulars gathered, where tourists stopped to snap pictures, where the air always carried the rich, smoky promise of something delicious waiting inside.

On a Friday night, the picnic tables out front would be full of families and friends, their conversations weaving through the air along with the smoke from the pit. Even now, a few customers lingered near the takeout window, the foil-wrapped promise of brisket and ribs clutched in their hands. Mae could imagine the sound of laughter, the scrape of chairs against the boards on the porch, the way this place had quickly become something familiar. Maybe not everything new was bad.

She barely had to drive another couple blocks before she reached the turn that led to her parents' gravel driveway. The familiar crunch beneath her tires sent a wave of something deep and bittersweet through her memory as the house came into view. It looked the same—modest, inviting, with its wide front porch and that old wooden swing still swaying in the breeze. The chipped paint on the railing, the neatly stacked firewood against the side, the screen door that she knew would creak when she opened it—all of it was a time capsule, a whisper of home.

But the flower beds... those told a different story.

Once, her mother had spent hours tending them, her hands forever stained with soil as she coaxed blooms from the rich earth. The hydrangeas had stood tall, their petals thick and bursting with color, and the roses had climbed the trellis in elegant spirals. Now, weeds had crept in, choking out the life that once flourished there. The colors had faded, the soil dry and neglected. The sight hit Mae harder than she expected, a quiet confirmation of how much had changed in her absence.

Beyond the neglected flower beds, she spotted something new—clusters of bluebonnets had sprung up along the fence line, their indigo petals swaying gently in the breeze. They hadn't been planted there, but some-how, they'd found their way home. A small, unexpected burst of color, thriving despite the neglect around them. Mae swallowed hard, touched by the quiet resilience of it.

She put the car in park and exhaled slowly. She was home. But home wasn't the same.

Mae cut the engine and sat for a moment, gripping the steering wheel tightly. The drive had been long, but it wasn't the miles that weighed on her—it was the uncertainty of what awaited her inside. Her dad's voice from their call yesterday echoed in her mind. He had sounded steady, but she knew him well enough to hear the strain beneath it. For as long as she could remember, he had been her anchor, a man who faced life's challenges with quiet strength. To hear even the smallest tremor in his voice unnerved her.

Finally, she forced herself out of the car, her boots crunching on the gravel driveway. She looked up at the house she had known since childhood, standing as sturdy and timeless as ever. The Colonial Revival home, with its soft green siding and deep red shutters, carried the quiet grace of another era. The steeply pitched roof, accented by a dormer window, framed the second floor like a watchful eye. A brick chimney rose from one side, a reminder of the winter nights spent by the fire, wrapped in thick blankets with cups of hot cocoa in hand.

The wide wraparound porch, supported by stately white columns, stretched across the front like open arms, its railing still strong despite the years. The old porch swing, slightly askew, hung from rusted chains, swaying gently in the breeze. She could almost hear its familiar creak, the rhythmic back-and-forth of summer nights spent beside her mother, whispering secrets and dreams into the humid air as they sipped sweet tea.

The worn planks of the steps groaned beneath her weight, and the rhythmic tap of her heels echoed across the wooden porch as she stepped forward. Before she could reach for the handle, the door swung open. Her father stood there, his broad frame filling the doorway. His face looked older, the lines deeper, and his eyes tired in a way Mae had never seen before.

"Mae," he said, his voice catching slightly as he pushed open the screen door and pulled her into a hug. It was brief and stiff, but it held a lifetime of unspoken emotion. "Glad you made it."

She nodded, her throat tight. "How is she?"

"Go on and see her," he said, stepping aside. His voice was rougher than usual, and he avoided her eyes. "She's been asking when you were going to be here all morning. I'll fix us some lunch while you two catch up."

Mae hesitated, watching as he retreated toward the kitchen. The scent of furniture polish and faint traces of cinnamon lingered in the air, a familiar warmth that made her reminisce her childhood. Her father, always the steady one, seemed diminished somehow. The sight of it left her unsettled.

Stepping inside, Mae felt an immediate contrast to the world she had left behind in New York. The deep mahogany paneling, exposed wooden beams, and rich earth-toned rugs filled the space with a weight of history, a stark departure from the sleek, modern sterility of her Manhattan apartment. In the living room, the brick fireplace flickered with low embers, casting a golden glow over the handcrafted Mission-style furniture—dark wood, heavy, timeless. An aged leather armchair sat beside a Tiffany-style lamp, its stained-glass shade casting warm, dappled light onto the woven Persian rug beneath it.

The scent of brewed coffee, aged wood, and a faint trace of lavender from her mother's linen lingered as she walked down the hall, her footsteps muffled by the Persian runner. A framed photograph of her parents on their wedding day hung near the dining room, alongside decorative plates and heirloom silver displayed meticulously in the built-in sideboard. She traced her fingers along the wainscoting as she moved toward her parents' bedroom, each detail a memory, each texture a reminder of home.

The house was eerily quiet except for the steady hum of medical equipment. Pushing the bedroom door open gently, Mae felt her breath hitch. The room was bathed in soft afternoon light, filtering through heavy floral drapes that framed the windows. Her mother lay propped up against the tall, carved headboard of a four-poster bed, her once-vibrant face pale but still radiating a quiet grace. The quilt draped over her lap—one Mae had seen her work on years ago—was a meticulous patchwork of deep reds, soft creams, and faded blues, each square a testament to her mother's patience and artistry.

Mae swallowed hard, stepping closer. The old oak dresser with its oval mirror held a collection of delicate porcelain figurines and a small glass dish filled with lavender sachets. Everything was exactly as she remem-bered it, preserved as though time had slowed within these walls.

"Mae," her mother's voice was soft but steady, a small smile forming on her lips.

Mae sat beside her, gripping her frail hand gently, and for the first time since she had arrived, she felt herself exhale.

"Mae," her mother repeated, her voice thin but warm. "You're here."

"Of course I'm here, Mom. How are you feeling?" Mae asked gently, brushing a wisp of hair from her mother's forehead.

Her mother chuckled weakly. "Oh, you know me. Still bossing everyone around from bed." She squeezed Mae's hand gently. "But don't you worry about me. Tell me about New York."

Mae smiled, though it felt forced. "New York's the same. Busy, noisy, exhausting. I've missed this place." Her voice cracked slightly, and her mother gave her a know-ing look.

"Mae, it's okay to be scared," her mom said, her tone steady despite her frailty. "But you've always been strong—stronger than you know. And right now, believe it or not, your dad needs you to be the strong one."

Mae nodded, swallowing hard. "I'll do my best."

"Your best has always been more than enough," her mother said, brushing a strand of hair from Mae's face. "Now, tell me—how long are you staying?"

"As long as you need me," Mae said firmly.

Her mother's smile widened, and for a moment, the weight on Mae's shoulders felt lighter. She tightened her grip on her mother's hand, grounding herself in its fading warmth.

"You must be tired," her mother said after a moment, her voice soft with concern. "You've had a long trip."

Mae shook her head. "I'm fine."

Her mother gave her a knowing look. "You won't be any good to me if you don't take care of yourself too. Go on—get some tea, or something to eat. I'll still be here when you come back. I'm exhausted now anyway, and I can barely keep my eyes open. It was a long night, and they kept poking and prodding me all night at the hospital."

Mae hesitated but knew her mother was right. Standing, she tucked the blanket around her mother's legs and leaned down to press a kiss to her forehead.

"Get some rest, Mom. I'll be back in a bit."

As Mae left the bedroom, she swiped at the lone tear escaping from the corner of her eye before making her way to the kitchen. From the hallway, a faint, muffled sound stopped her in her tracks—her father's quiet sobs. She froze, her hand resting against the wall.

She had never seen or heard her father cry before, and the realization struck her like a blow. Her father—the man who had always been her steady ground, her unshakable force—was breaking. And for a moment, she didn't know what to do. Giving him the space he probably needed, she stayed where she was, letting the raw emotion settle before stepping into the kitchen.

The space was warm and familiar, the scent of fresh coffee lingering in the air. Exposed wooden beams stretched across the ceiling, complementing the deep cherry wood cabinets and wainscoting that lined the walls. Soft amber light glowed from the vintage-style lanterns hanging above the kitchen island, casting gentle shadows over the stone countertops. The blue-gray cabinets added a subdued contrast, and the farmhouse sink sat beneath a wide window that framed the sprawling backyard. Everything about the kitchen felt solid, lived-in—unchanged, even as everything else in Mae's world felt uncertain.

Mae cleared her throat gently as she stepped inside. "She's resting now," she said, keeping her voice even. "Told me I needed to get some food in me."

Her father stood at the counter, quickly swiping a hand over his face before turning to her with a forced smile. "Oh, good. I'm sure she's exhausted. Lunch is almost ready. Just sandwiches and some chips—hope that's okay."

Mae nodded, pretending not to notice the redness in his eyes. "Sounds perfect, Dad."

The sandwiches were simple, made with homemade bread from a neighbor, but Mae savored the small act of normalcy. As they ate, the silence between them felt heavy, but not uncomfortable. It was her father who broke it first, his voice low and steady.

"She's been through a lot in the past forty-eight hours," he said, his gaze fixed on the sandwich in his hands. "But she's tough. Tougher than me."

Mae looked up, surprised to see his eyes glistening again. She hadn't seen him cry before today, and the sight unraveled something in her. "Dad..."

He shook his head quickly, regaining composure. "Sorry. I just... I'm glad you're here. We've had so much help from folks around town. The Stevensons brought over that bread this morning, and the church is already organizing a dinner schedule. I think half the town's signed up to drop off meals. You know how they are—nobody in Twinsdale goes through something like this alone."

Mae blinked, letting his words settle. The thought of an entire community rallying around her parents filled her with equal parts gratitude and guilt. In New York, neighbors barely exchanged nods in the hallway, let alone coordinated meal trains. Here, word traveled fast—often faster than the family could speak it themselves. It was a kind of care and connection that felt foreign to her now, though she had once taken it for granted and, at times, wished for just a bit more privacy.

"It's different," Mae said softly. "The way people show up here. In New York, it's just... not like this."

Her father nodded, the corners of his mouth lifting in a faint, bittersweet smile. "It's a good town. Your mom always said that when things get hard, the people here show up. Every time."

Mae nodded, her throat tightening. "I see that now." She suddenly felt a sense of belonging—like she was exactly where she needed to be.

As Mae lingered at the kitchen table, her father busied himself with the small, methodical tasks of cleaning up their meal. The faint clatter of dishes and the hiss of water from the faucet filled the silence, grounding her in the familiar rhythm of home. The scent of fresh bread and mustard still lingered in the air, mingling with the faint smell of dish soap. The wooden floor creaked under her father's slow, deliberate movements, the same way it had when she was a child sneaking into the kitchen late at night for a glass of water. She used to believe the house itself could sense every movement, whispering its memories through the groans of its old bones.

Mae watched her father from across the room, his broad shoulders slightly hunched, his movements deliberate but slower than she remembered. The man who once tossed her effortlessly into the air now seemed to carry an invisible weight, pressing down on him with each passing year. Time had softened him in ways she hadn't noticed until now. The kitchen, too, bore quiet marks of change—newer curtains framing the window, slightly mismatched plates in the drying rack, the absence of her mother's humming that once filled every quiet space.

"Want some help with that?" Mae finally asked, standing and gesturing toward the sink.

Her father glanced over his shoulder and shrugged. "If you want to dry, I won't stop you."

Mae grabbed a dishtowel and joined him at the counter. For a while, they worked in silence, the only sounds the scrape of a plate against porcelain and the soft whoosh of the dish towel. The steady rhythm of it, the quiet teamwork, reminded her of childhood nights when she stood on a step stool to dry the dishes, eager to prove she was grown up enough to help.

"You know," her dad said eventually, his voice low, "your mom always said you had a way of making people feel like they belonged. Even when you were little, you'd pull the neighborhood kids together, make sure no one got left out."

Mae smiled faintly. "I remember that. It was always a hassle keeping Jimmy Tucker from wandering off. But I couldn't stand seeing anyone sit alone."

Her father chuckled softly, the sound catching her off guard. It was the first time she'd heard him laugh since her arrival. "That's just who you are, Mae. You keep people together. You always have."

A warmth spread through her, unexpected but welcome. She had spent so much time believing she had left that part of herself behind—that in New York, survival meant looking out for herself first. But maybe, just maybe, she had been wrong about that.

"You've got that same gift now," he said, his tone more serious. "And we're going to need it."

Mae paused, gripping the towel tightly. A familiar knot formed in her throat, the same one that always came when she thought too hard about what was happening—about her mother, about her father's quiet exhaustion, about the way home felt both comforting and fragile all at once.

"Dad, you don't have to carry this alone," she said, her voice softer than she intended. "I'm here. Whatever you need, we'll figure it out."

Her father dried his hands and leaned against the counter, meeting her gaze. His eyes, weathered by time and worry, held something unspoken—gratitude, love, the weight of too many sleepless nights.

"I know you will, Mae," he said. "I don't say it enough, but I'm proud of you. Always have been."

The weight of his words settled over her, heavy and comforting all at once. Mae swallowed hard and nodded, unsure how to respond. The lump in her throat made words impossible, so she simply held onto the moment, tucking it away like a pressed flower in a book, something to return to when she needed it most.

And then, before she could second-guess herself, she stepped forward and wrapped her arms around him, pressing her cheek against his chest. He stiffened for half a second, as if caught off guard, then exhaled and hugged her back, his arms strong and steady around her.

For a moment, she wasn't an adult carrying the weight of too many responsibilities. She was just a little girl again, safe in her father's arms, her face buried in the scent of soap and faint traces of sawdust that always clung to his clothes. She could almost hear the echoes of childhood—the way he used to scoop her up effortlessly, spinning her in the air until she shrieked with laughter.

She closed her eyes, holding on just a little longer.

Her dad let out a long breath, rubbing a hand over his face. The exhaustion in his eyes was unmistakable, the kind that settled deep in a person's bones. "You should get some rest," he said, glancing at her with concern. "You've been traveling all day."

Mae shook her head. "I'm fine," she insisted. "But you look like you could use some sleep."

He gave a small huff, as if debating whether to argue, but then let it go with a tired nod. "Maybe you're right."

She hesitated for a moment, then glanced toward the kitchen. "I was thinking about heading into town. Grabbing some pralines for Mom. She always loved the ones from Sally's."

Her father's lips curled into a small, knowing smile. "She'd like that."

Mae grabbed her keys, feeling a sense of purpose settle over her. This was something she could do—something small, but meaningful. A way to bring a little comfort to her mother.

As she stepped outside and into the warm evening air, she realized something else, too. She wasn't just running an errand. She was stepping back into this town, into the life she had left behind.

# Chapter 5

# Nostalgia

Mae eased her car down the quiet backstreets of Twinsdale, her fingers light on the steering wheel as she soaked in the town's unchanged charm. The roads were lined with sprawling oaks, their branches just beginning to bud with the first hints of spring. The air carried the faintest scent of fresh earth and distant barbecue smoke, the kind of aroma that settled into the bones of this town like an old friend.

As she pulled onto Main Street and stepped out of her car, she let herself linger in the moment. The town looked almost exactly as she had left it all those years ago. The brick buildings, many standing for over a century, bore the familiar wear of time but remained resilient. Their striped awnings cast long afternoon shadows, and the golden sunlight bathed everything in a nostalgic glow. The distant whistle of a diesel truck mixed with the occasional bark of a dog and the soft chime of a storefront bell, creating a melody she hadn't realized she missed.

She started walking, her Prada calfskin loafers click-ing softly against the uneven pavement, taking in the details that made this place home. Dressed in dark-wash designer jeans that hugged her frame perfectly and a terracotta University of Texas sweatshirt, she felt both at ease and strangely out of place—like a missing puzzle piece suddenly returned to its original set.

The tiny movie theater's retro marquee still pro-claimed **Friday Night Classics**, though a few bulbs were clearly burnt out. *Grease* was the feature this week. A few doors down, the hardware store displayed a weathered sign advertising a **Spring Garden Sale**, and just beyond it, The Lone Star Café, the local diner still boasted *the best chicken fried steak in Texas* on its handwritten chalkboard menu. The familiar sights tugged at something deep within her, as though she had stepped into a preserved memory where time hadn't dared to move too quickly.

As she neared the post office, Mae spotted a small group of older women gathered near the front steps, their conversation quieting as they noticed her approach. They were longtime friends of her mother—pillars of the community whose lives were woven into the very fabric of this town. Their smiles were warm, but their eyes carried the weight of knowing more than they let on.

"Mae Whitaker," one of them called out, her voice bright yet gentle. Mrs. Peterson, the grocer's wife and one of her mother's closest friends, stepped forward. "Well, honey, it's been too long."

Mae slowed to a stop, returning the small smile. "Hi, Mrs. Peterson. It's good to see you."

The women drew closer, their presence a familiar cocoon of care. Mrs. Peterson reached for Mae's hand, giving it a reassuring squeeze. "We've all been thinking about your mama. You know how much she means to us—between teaching Sunday school and organizing the book drive at the library, that woman's touched more lives than she knows. She's in our prayers, sweetheart. And if you or your family need anything, you let us know, alright? Anything at all."

Mae nodded, her throat tightening. "Thank you. That means a lot."

She took in the sight of them—dressed in stylish but practical layers, their Grantets buttoned against the crisp afternoon air. Mrs. Peterson wore a fitted black coat with a silk scarf elegantly draped around her neck, her salt-and-pepper hair perfectly coiffed. Beside her, Mrs. Cunningham sported a cheerful pink trench coat, her well-worn boots peeking from beneath dark jeans. Mrs. Harris had chosen a robin's egg blue Grantet, her arm linked through that of Mrs. Thompson, who was wrapped in a cozy black puffer. The last of the group, Mrs. Fields, stood with a quiet but confident presence in a sleek leather Grantet, the epitome of no-nonsense grace.

They were the picture of small-town resilience—women who had weathered life's storms together, their friendships etched into the very essence of this town. Mae felt the warmth of home settling over her, unexpected yet deeply familiar.

Mrs. Fields offered a knowing smile. "Your mama's one of the strongest women I know. She always talks about how proud she is of you, Mae. Brags about you every chance she gets—says you're doing big things in New York," her fist rising in triumph as she flashed a bright smile of encouragement.

Mae blinked back the unexpected sting of tears, managing a small, wistful smile. "She always did have a way of making things sound more impressive than they really are."

The women laughed softly, their presence like a gentle embrace. They didn't linger long, sensing Mae's need for space, but as they continued down the street, their warmth remained—a quiet reassurance that she and her family weren't alone.

As Mae wandered further, a few men tipped their hats or offered curt nods of acknowledgment. These were her father's friends—men who had coached alongside him, worked on town projects, or watched Mae grow up from behind the counter of their own small businesses. Their gestures were subtle but carried weight, the quiet strength of men who didn't need words to convey their concern.

Mae felt both comforted and overwhelmed by the attention. In New York, she could disappear into a sea of strangers, her anonymity a protective shield. Here, everyone knew her name, her family, her history. And though the contrast was stark, it reminded her of a closeness she hadn't realized she missed.

A sudden feeling of belonging began to swell from within—not just belonging to a city or a job, but to something much deeper. Almost as if she belonged to the community of people who had always been here, waiting for her to find her way back home.

The bell above the door jingled as Mae stepped into Sally's Sweet Shop, and the scent of sugar, butter, and roasted pecans wrapped around her like a warm embrace. It pulled her straight back to childhood afternoons spent here with her mother, fingers sticky from pralines, laughter spilling between bites of homemade fudge. The wooden floors creaked beneath her feet, each step a familiar note in a melody she hadn't heard in years. Sunlight filtered through the red-and-white checkered curtains, casting a golden glow over the rustic space.

The shop looked just as it always had—wooden barrels brimming with old-fashioned candy, shelves lined with glass jars filled with colorful treats, and a worn wooden table piled high with neatly wrapped confections. The glass display case at the counter showcased Sally's signature chocolates, each one a tiny masterpiece dusted with cocoa or drizzled with caramel. This place wasn't just a store; it was a piece of the town's heart, beating steadily despite the passing years.

Behind the counter, Sally stood just as spry as Mae remembered. Her short platinum hair was styled in a chic, no-nonsense cut that suited her vibrant personality. Dressed in a crisp white blouse and a well-worn red apron dusted with flour, she exuded the warmth of someone who had spent a lifetime perfecting the art of sweetness—in her confections and her company. Her sharp blue eyes sparkled as she looked up, recognizing Mae instantly.

"Well, if it isn't Mae Whitaker!" Sally exclaimed, wiping her hands on her apron. Her voice carried the same comforting warmth it always had, like honey drizzled over a fresh-baked biscuit. "How long's it been, honey? You're a sight for sore eyes. Come over here and give me a hug."

Mae smiled, the genuine affection in Sally's voice easing a tension she hadn't even realized she was carrying. She stepped forward, wrapping her arms around the woman who had once slipped her extra caramel clusters when her mother wasn't looking. The embrace smelled of vanilla and powdered sugar, familiar and grounding.

"Too long, Sally," Mae said, pulling back. "How've you been?"

"Oh, you know me," Sally said with a wink. "This place keeps me on my toes." She leaned on the counter, her expression softening. "I heard about your mama, honey. I'm so sorry. How's she doin'?"

Mae swallowed past the lump in her throat, the scent of warm pralines and chocolate-covered pretzels stirring up bittersweet memories. "Thank you. It's... a lot to take in."

Sally nodded, reaching across the counter to give Mae's hand a gentle squeeze. "Well, you just let me know if you need anything, sweetheart. And before you go, I won't let you leave without a bag of your mama's favorites."

Mae let out a soft laugh, the warmth of this place settling deep in her bones. Some things, thankfully, never changed. But as she reached for the small box, her smile faltered. "Thank you, Sally. It means a lot. How'd you know that's what I came in for?"

Sally's eyes twinkled. "Your mama's a special lady, Mae. Did you know she brags about you every chance she gets? Every time she comes in here, she's talkin' 'bout how proud she is of the strong, independent woman you've become. Said you're proof that a little girl from Twinsdale could make it big."

Mae's throat tightened, the unexpected praise filling her with equal parts pride and guilt. "She really said that?"

"Every time." Sally slid the box of pecan pralines across the counter with a knowing smile. "And don't you forget it, darlin'. Now, take these to her and tell her I'm thinking of her, alright?"

Mae nodded, her voice barely above a whisper. "I will. Thank you, Sally. You always know just what to say." She reached for her wallet. "What do I owe you?"

Sally waved her off. "On the house, honey. Now, what about you? Can I get you anything?"

Mae shook her head, a soft smile returning to her lips. "Nothing for me this time around, but I'll be back for a big ice cream cone soon. Just like old times."

As Mae stepped back onto the sidewalk, pralines in hand, the scent of post oak smoke drifted through the air, rich and unmistakable. Her gaze followed it to Rocket Ribs and BBQ across the street, where the patio buzzed with diners enjoying late lunches. By the massive smoker, tending to the pit with the ease of a man who knew exactly what he was doing, stood Jim Carter.

She had known he was back in Twinsdale. It was hard not to, with how often his name had come up in her parents' calls. But hearing about him and seeing him were two different things. Time had only sharpened his features, turning the boy she once admired from afar into a man who carried himself with effortless confidence. She had always thought of him as out of reach back in high school—four years older, too cool, too good-looking. But now, as he stood there, broad-shouldered and sure, covered in a dusting of wood smoke and ash, she realized she still felt that same flutter in her chest. And she hated that he could still have that effect on her after all these years.

"Mae Whitaker? That you?" Jim's voice carried across the street, a mix of surprise and warmth.

Mae turned, a small smile tugging at her lips. "Jim Carter. Long time." Without thinking, she stepped off the curb and crossed the street, the pralines tucked securely under her arm. The heat from the pavement radiated upward, mixing with the scent of smoke and spice as she neared the restaurant.

"Fifteen years, give or take," Jim said, stepping closer. Up close, he was every bit as striking as she remembered, but the years had carved something deeper into him. The boyish charm of the high school quarterback had evolved into a rugged, effortless confidence. His frame was broader, solid with the kind of strength earned from years of military service at the highest levels of expertise. His fitted T-shirt clung to powerful shoulders and arms, dusted with a fine layer of ash, a testament to hours spent by the fire. Flecks of charcoal clung to the stubble along his jaw, and his tanned skin bore the faint lines of someone who lived under the Texas sun. Yet, his eyes—warm, steady, and just a little teasing—hadn't changed at all.

A black cap sat low on his forehead, embroidered with the Black Rifle Coffee logo, the brim curved and tattered from years of wear. He studied her, his smirk unreadable yet familiar, as though time had never fully separated them.

"Didn't expect to see you back in Twinsdale," Jim said, taking a slow sip from the steaming coffee in his hand. "You hungry?"

"I just ate," Mae replied, lifting the box in her hand. "But I couldn't pass up Sally's pralines."

He chuckled, nodding toward the shop. "Good choice. Best pralines in Texas, hands down. You want some coffee to go with that?"

Mae hesitated, then nodded. "Sure, why not? I missed my cup of joe this morning on the way in, and I could use a little caffeine at this point."

Jim motioned her toward the patio, leading her to a table near the smoker, where the scent of slow-cooked brisket hung in the air. As she settled into her chair, she studied him, taking in the details of the man he had become.

"How'd you even recognize me after all this time?"

Jim grinned, leaning back in his chair. "Your parents. They come by the restaurant a lot, and your mom shows me pictures every time. Hard to forget when she talks about you like you hung the moon."

Mae laughed softly, the warmth of his words sinking in. "That sounds like her. By the way, I saw in the Gazette that you'd come back to Twinsdale. People have been saying great things about your barbecue."

"Appreciate that," Jim said, his expression thoughtful. "After spending a decade overseas, I was ready for a change. Slower pace, good food, familiar faces—it's been good for me."

Mae nodded, nostalgia stirring. "It's good to see you, Jim."

You too, Mae," he said, his gaze steady. For a moment, the years between them seemed to fade, replaced by the comforting familiarity of home.

The view from the patio stretched beyond the smoker, rolling hills bathed in the golden glow of the afternoon sun. The light softened everything, painting the fields in warm amber tones, casting long shadows that stretched toward the horizon. Clusters of bluebonnets dotted the hills, their vibrant indigo petals swaying gently in the breeze, adding a touch of wild beauty to the landscape. The scent of post oak smoke drifted lazily through the air, mingling with the rich aroma of barbecue and freshly brewed coffee.

Jim disappeared inside for a moment and returned with two steaming mugs, a small dish of sugar and cream balanced on the tray. Setting it in front of her, he grinned.

"I had a feeling you weren't the black coffee type," he said, sliding the sugar and cream toward her.

Mae laughed, shaking her head as she reached for the sugar. "You guessed right. If I can't make it taste like dessert, I'm out."

Jim smirked, cradling his own mug as she stirred a generous amount of cream and sugar into hers. "Some things don't change," he mused.

Mae arched a brow playfully. "And some things do," she countered, nodding toward the smoker and the carefully arranged tables on the patio. "You've got quite the setup here. It's a good spot."

"Best view in town," Jim agreed, tipping his head toward the hills in the distance. "Nothing beats watching the sunrise while the smoker gets going."

Mae followed his gaze, taking in the rolling landscape, the way the soft light kissed the fields, making them glow as if lit from within. She lifted her mug, taking a slow sip, the warmth of the coffee spreading through her, the sweet richness settling on her tongue. "I can see why you came back," she admitted, her voice softer now, more reflective.

Jim studied her for a moment, his expression unreadable. "And what about you?" he asked. "What's got you back in Twinsdale?"

Mae hesitated, the weight of her mother's illness pressing against her chest, tightening her throat. She wasn't ready to say it out loud—not yet. So she offered a small, practiced smile instead. "Family stuff," she said finally. "It was time to come home for a bit."

Jim nodded, a quiet understanding in his eyes, as though he sensed there was more she wasn't saying. But he didn't press. Instead, he leaned back in his chair, his fingers tracing the rim of his coffee mug. "Well, it's good to see you, Mae. It's been a long time."

"It has," she murmured, meeting his gaze. For a moment, the noise of the world seemed to fade—the hum of distant conversation, the clatter of dishes, the rustling breeze through the oak trees. There was only the two of them, the scent of post oak smoke curling in the air, the warmth of coffee between their hands.

Mae took another sip, savoring the sweetness, and let herself relax—if only for a moment.

# Chapter 6

# Coffee and Conversation

Mae sat in the warmth of the sun, her hands wrapped around the steaming mug of coffee Jim had just set in front of her. The faint scent of smoked brisket lingered in the air, mingling with hints of cedarwood from the deck boards and something earthy she couldn't quite place. It was comforting, grounding—like everything else about this place. The patio, with its weathered picnic tables and string lights that would glow softly come evening, overlooked rolling hills bathed in golden light. At the edge of the deck, the smoker released faint, thin curls of transparently blue smoke, a testament to the craft Jim had clearly mastered. Beyond that, wild bluebonnets swayed in the breeze, their indigo petals painting the fields with a vibrancy that made her heart ache with nostalgia.

She glanced back inside the restaurant through the opened French patio doors. The barnwood walls were adorned with rusted Texas license plates and old local road signs, their faded colors telling stories of roads well-traveled. Cowboy hats, some nearly crushed with wear and ringed with white sweat marks, hung from hooks beside the door. The scuffed wooden floor bore the marks of countless boots, while the bar—a dark, gleaming relic from the early 1900s—stood proudly beneath the dim, golden glow of pendant lights. Jim's touch was everywhere, from the framed art pieces of Texas landscapes and fields of bluebonnets to the Corona bottle salt and pepper shakers on each table. It felt like a place meant to be lived in, not just visited.

Jim leaned casually against the edge of the chair across from her. "So, what do you think of the place? Be honest," he said, his tone light, but his expression betraying a hint of nerves.

Mae took a slow sip of her coffee, her gaze sweeping over the space again. "It's..." She hesitated, searching for the right word, before the truth slipped out. "It's perfect. It feels like home. Like it's lived a life."

Jim's shoulders relaxed, and a small, pleased smile curved his lips. "That's what I was going for. I wanted people to feel like they could just walk in, sit down, and take a breather. Glad to know I'm hitting the mark."

Mae glanced toward the smoker, then back at her coffee cup. "You know, you smoke just about everything else—ribs, brisket, peaches... I'm surprised you haven't tried smoking coffee."

Jim's eyebrows lifted, his smile widening with interest. "Smoked coffee?" he repeated, sitting up straighter. "Now *that's* actually a great idea."

Mae chuckled. "I was kidding."

"I'm not," he said, already lost in thought. "That could be incredible. Bold, smooth, maybe a hint of cherry wood or hickory? That's genius."

Mae shook her head, laughing softly. "I've created a monster."

Jim grinned. "Just wait. If it turns out to be the best thing I've ever made, I'm naming it after you. Mae's Mid-night Roast."

"Oh no," she groaned playfully. "I regret mentioning already."

Jim laughed again, clearly energized by the idea.

Mae traced the rim of her mug with her fingertip, glancing up at him through her lashes. "You've definitely got the Texas charm thing down. It's almost unfair."

Jim laughed softly, shaking his head. "I don't know about unfair. But I'll take that as a compliment."

Mae leaned back slightly in her chair, her lips quirking into a faint smile. "It was meant as one. I'll admit, I didn't expect you to turn out to be the kind of guy who runs a place like this. High school Jim Carter was all about football and charm, but this... this feels different. Authentic."

Jim raised an eyebrow, his grin turning playful. "Oh, so you were paying attention to me in high school?"

Mae's cheeks warmed slightly, but she held his gaze. "Don't flatter yourself, Carter. Everyone was paying attention to you."

"Touché," he said, his grin widening.

Their conversation hung there for a moment, the air between them lighter but charged with something unspoken. Mae felt a flicker of something she hadn't felt in a long time—a mixture of ease and intrigue. She took another sip of her coffee, letting the warmth spread through her.

Jim leaned forward slightly, resting his elbows on the table. "So, what's life like in the big city? I've only been to New York once, and that was years ago. Too crowded for my taste."

Mae shrugged, swirling her coffee idly. "It's busy. Always something going on, somewhere to be. It's exciting... but it can also be a little overwhelming. Sometimes it feels like there's never enough time to just sit still."

Jim studied her for a moment, his expression softening. "Sounds like you could use more moments like this. Sitting still. Taking a breather."

Mae glanced up at him, surprised by the quiet sincerity in his tone. "Yeah," she admitted, her voice quieter now. "It's been a long time since I've taken a breather."

Jim nodded, his gaze steady. "Well, for what it's worth, you're always welcome here. No pressure, no rush. Just coffee, barbecue, and good company."

Mae smiled, a small, genuine one that caught her off guard. "That's a pretty good sales pitch, Carter."

"I've been told I'm persuasive," he said with a wink.

The faint buzz of Mae's phone interrupted the moment. She glanced at the screen and saw her dad's name. Her smile faded as she answered. "Hey, Dad," she said, her voice soft.

Her father's voice on the other end was calm but tinged with urgency. "Mae, the doctor's here, and he'd like to talk to both of us. Can you come home?"

Mae's heart sank. "Of course. I'll be right there."

She ended the call and turned to Jim, who had been watching her closely. He straightened, his casual posture shifting to one of quiet concern as he noticed a tenseness come over her.

"Everything okay?" he asked gently.

Mae forced a small smile, slipping her phone back into her pocket. "My dad needs me back at the house. What do I owe you for the coffee?"

Jim nodded, his gaze searching hers for a moment before he stepped aside. "Coffee's on the house today, but hey," he said, his voice teasing yet kind, "if I'd known you were going to leave so soon, I'd have brought out the big guns—like the smoked peach cobbler. That always gets people to stick around."

Mae smiled despite the weight pressing on her chest. "Next time, lead with dessert. That's how you win me over."

"Noted," Jim replied with mock seriousness, acting as though he was writing the suggestion down on an invisible notepad, his grin widening. "But fair warning, once you try it, you'll be coming back every day. It's been known to cause cobbler addiction."

Mae laughed softly, shaking her head. "You're ridiculous."

Jim leaned in slightly, a spark of playful energy lighting his expression. "Also, I meant what I said earlier—I'm seriously going to try that smoked coffee idea. You may have just changed the game, Whitaker."

Mae blinked, caught off guard by the earnestness in his voice. She wasn't sure if he was teasing or not—but the thought of it made her heart flicker in a strange, unexpected way.

Her laughter faded, replaced by something quieter and warmer. The sincerity in his eyes, the steady reassurance in his voice, settled into her like a quiet comfort she hadn't realized she needed.

"Thanks for the coffee, Jim. I appreciate it."

As she stepped off the patio and across the street, she stole one last glance back at him. His playful smirk was still there, but as she climbed into her car and pulled away, she caught him in the rearview mirror—still watching her, his gaze lingering like he wasn't quite ready for her to leave.

Mae gripped the wheel a little tighter, her pulse flickering at the memory of his easy smile, the warmth of his voice. She told herself it was nothing—just nostalgia, just small-town familiarity. But deep down, she felt the quiet unraveling of something she thought she had long since outgrown— a pull, a warmth, a gentle ache she couldn't quite name that made her wonder if she was finally allowing herself to entertain what had always felt just out of reach.

Because as much as she had tried to convince herself otherwise, Jim Carter still made her heart race like she was seventeen again.

# Chapter 7

# Crossroads

Mae entered the living room slowly, her eyes immediately finding her father, John, sitting stiffly in his recliner. His hands gripped the armrests as though they were the only things keeping him tethered. His gaze darted to the back door, then back to the floor, his shoulders tight with tension. Mae had never seen him like this before—her father, the man who always had a plan, now sitting in silence, lost and disoriented. The sight sent a pang through her chest.

Standing nearby was Dr. Abbott, his medical bag resting on the floor. He had been in their lives for as long as Mae could remember, not just as the town doctor but as her father's best friend. There was a gravity in his posture, the weight of difficult truths hanging between them. He turned as Mae entered, his expression soft-ening.

"Mae," Dr. Abbott said gently, nodding in acknowledgement.

Mae offered a small smile, though her heart pounded in her chest. She moved toward her father, resting a hand on his shoulder in a silent offering of comfort. He didn't react, his fingers flexing against the worn fabric of the chair, his focus still locked on the floor. With a quiet exhale, Mae stepped around the recliner and lowered herself onto the couch. Her hands clasped tightly in her lap as she glanced at her father. He avoided her gaze, his silence heavier than words.

"Let's sit," Dr. Abbott said, his voice kind but steady. He took a seat across from them, folding his hands together.

Mae listened as Dr. Abbott began to speak. His words were measured, clinical at first—hospice care, palliative measures, final days—but his tone softened as he shifted from doctor to family friend.

"Sandy has always been one of the strongest women I've ever known," he said, his voice cracking slightly. "She's faced this with grace and courage, but... it's her time now. Her heart failure, caused by a condition called dilated cardiomyopathy, has reached its final stage. We managed it for a long time, but sometimes the decline comes quickly."

The room seemed to close in on Mae. She blinked rapidly, willing herself to stay composed, even as memories of her mother's strength flooded her mind—mom, teaching her how to bake cookies; mom, cheering the loudest at every one of her basketball games; mom, holding her close after her first heartbreak, whispering that she would survive it. The thought of a world without her mother in it felt impossible.

Her father's hands tightened on the chair. For a moment, Mae thought he might speak, but instead, he rose abruptly. "Excuse me," he muttered, his voice tight and strained. He strode toward the back door, his steps quick and uneven, and disappeared outside.

Mae watched him go, her chest tightening. He'd always been the one with the plan, the strategy to conquer and overcome. Now, he was lost, unmoored by the one thing he couldn't fix. Mae's instinct was to follow him, to offer the kind of comfort he had always given her, but she knew he needed space.

"Thank you," she said quietly, turning back to Dr. Abbott. Her voice was steady, but her hands trembled in her lap. "Thank you for everything you've done for her."

Dr. Abbott nodded, his own eyes glistening. "Your dad's going to need you, Mae," he said, his voice soft. "He's been my best friend since we were kids, but even I can't carry this for him. You'll need to be his anchor."

Mae swallowed hard, her throat burning. "I know," she whispered. "And I will."

Dr. Abbott hesitated for a moment, then glanced toward the backyard. "I'll go check on him. Give him a moment to breathe."

As the doctor stepped outside, Mae remained on the couch for a long moment, her fingers pressing into her lap as if grounding herself could keep the emotions at bay. A tidal wave of grief threatened to crash over her, its weight pressing against her chest, but she couldn't let it consume her—not now. She wanted to cry, to let it all out, but instead, she forced herself to go still. To go numb.

She sat frozen for a moment, the silence in the room deafening. Her brain scrambled to find something to do, something to say—anything but sit with the ache that was threatening to unspool her from the inside out. She didn't know how to talk to her mother about this. She didn't even know how to begin. If she let herself go there—if she let the grief crack open, even a little—it would all come pouring out.

Instead, she latched onto the safest impulse she could find: change the subject, play it light, pretend for a little while longer. Her mother deserved joy in these moments, not fear. Mae could unravel later. Right now, she had to smile. She had to be strong.

She inhaled deeply, slow and deliberate, as if drawing in strength with each breath. In her mind, she took the news—the ache of it, the weight—and placed it in a box, small and heavy. She imagined sealing it shut, locking it tight, and sliding it into the farthest corner of herself, where it couldn't touch the surface. Not yet. She would open it later, when she had the space to fall apart. But right now, she couldn't afford to. With quiet resolve, she squared her shoulders and pushed herself to her feet.

The hallway stretched before her, each step feeling heavier, like she was wading through something thick and unrelenting. She kept reminding herself, over and over she couldn't afford to break. Not now. Not yet. Her parents needed her. Her mother needed her. Just as they had stood by her through every battle she had fought, she would be strong for them now.

So she walked forward, one step at a time, shutting the door on her own emotions, locking them away where they couldn't reach her—where they couldn't make her crumble.

The hum of medical equipment greeted Mae as she entered her mother's bedroom. The faint beeps and whirs filled the quiet, but the room still felt warm, lived-in. Sunlight filtered through the lace curtains, casting soft patterns on the quilt that draped over Sandy's frail frame. Photographs lined the shelves—black-and-white snap-shots of her parents' wedding, sunlit pictures of Mae as a child, and even a recent photo from her last Christmas visit three years ago. An open photo album rested on the nightstand, its pages turned to images of summer vacations and family gatherings. The memories were almost tangible, wrapping around Mae like a blanket.

Despite the frailty of the woman in the bed, Sandy's eyes lit up as Mae approached.

"Mae, sweetheart," her mom said weakly, her smile as bright as ever.

Mae forced a cheerful smile as she sat on the edge of the bed. "Guess what I brought you?" She pulled out the box of pecan pralines from Sally's Sweet Shop and placed them on the nightstand.

"Oh, you didn't," Sandy said, her laughter soft but genuine. "I haven't had these in months."

"I figured you deserved a treat," Mae said, unwrapping one and handing it to her. "Besides, I needed to bribe you to get your advice about the craziest thing that happened today."

Her mom raised an eyebrow, her amusement clear. "This I have to hear."

Mae leaned closer, her tone playful. "I ran into Jim Carter."

"Jim Carter, you say?" Sandy said, her eyes sparkling with interest. "Well, how's he doing?"

"Oh, he's doing fine. I got to see Rocket Ribs and BBQ today—and it's incredible. The whole place feels like a slice of Texas history." Mae paused, watching the way her mother's eyes lit up with pride before she added, "But you'll love this: he recognized me because of you," as she poked her mom with her forefinger in a playful way.

Sandy's smile turned mischievous. "Because of me?"

Mae smirked. "Apparently, you've been showing him pictures of me every time you visit the restaurant. Care to explain?"

Sandy chuckled, clearly unbothered. "Well, I can't help it if I'm a proud mama. He asked about you once, and I figured, why not show him how great you're doing in New York?"

Mae laughed, shaking her head. "Mom, you do realize how embarrassing that is, right? He even told me you make me sound like I hung the moon."

"Well, haven't you?" Sandy teased, taking another bite of praline. Her expression turned a little more serious, though her smile remained. "Truth be told, I've always thought Jim was a fine young man. And if I'm being honest, I always hoped the two of you might end up together one day."

Mae nearly choked on air. "Mom! Where is this coming from?"

Sandy's eyes twinkled with mischief. "Oh, come on, Mae. You two always had something special, even back in high school. Don't act like you didn't notice."

Mae's cheeks burned. "We haven't seen each other in fifteen years! Whatever you thought was there is ancient history."

"Maybe," Sandy said with a shrug, her voice light but pointed. "But sometimes, history has a funny way of repeating itself."

Mae shook her head, though she couldn't help the small laugh that escaped. "You're incorrigible."

"Just saying what's on my mind, sweetheart," Sandy said, reaching for her hand. "Life's funny like that. The things we think are behind us often find their way back when we least expect it."

Mae didn't respond, but her mother's words lingered, planting a seed she wasn't quite ready to examine.

The sound of the doorbell interrupted their moment, and Mae sighed. "I'll get it," she said, standing quickly. Her caretaker instincts kicked in immediately, knowing her father was still outside with Dr. Abbott.

She paused at the doorway, glancing back at her mother. Sandy gave her a small smile, her eyes warm. "Bring me another praline when you're done."

Mae laughed softly, her heart feeling lighter as she headed downstairs.

# Chapter 8

# Reflections

The doorbell's chime echoed through the house as Mae descended the stairs. She opened the door to find Pastor Terry and his wife, Dara, standing on the porch, each holding an armful of food. The aroma of homemade lasagna hit Mae instantly, bringing a warmth that cut through the heavy day.

"Mae!" Dara greeted warmly, shifting the foil-covered dish in her hands and reaching in for a one armed hug. "We thought you all could use a little help tonight."

Pastor Terry smiled, balancing a large pitcher of sweet tea and a basket of garlic bread. "Dinner's on us. And, of course, we're here for anything else you might need."

Mae stepped aside, gesturing them in. "You didn't have to do all this, but thank you. It smells amazing."

"Your mom and dad have done so much for this community," Dara said, setting the food on the kitchen counter. "It's the least we can do to give back."

Before Mae could respond, the back door opened, and her dad walked in with Dr. Abbott in tow. The two men were deep in conversation but stopped when they saw the scene unfolding in the kitchen.

"Well, if it isn't an impromptu feast," her dad said with a small smile, as he reached to shake Terry's hand. "What do we owe the pleasure?"

"Just a little love from your church family," Pastor Terry replied, clapping him on the shoulder. "Thought we'd bring dinner and maybe a little encouragement."

Mae noticed her dad's shoulders relax slightly as he nodded. "That's mighty kind of you."

"It's what we're here for," Pastor Terry said, his tone gentle.

Before long, everyone found themselves in Sandy's bedroom. The bed was adjusted so she could sit up, and Dara carefully balanced a plate of lasagna on the nightstand for her. The rest of the group settled in wherever they could find space—the recliner in the corner, chairs from the dining room, even the edge of the bed.

Sandy's room, like the rest of the house, was a testament to her and John's deep faith. A framed painting of Jesus hung above the bed, and a small wooden cross sat on her nightstand next to a well-worn Bible, its pages marked with church bulletins and sticky notes. On the dresser, a collection of family photos shared space with a figurine of the Last Supper.

The room filled with the sound of quiet conversation and the clink of forks on plates. For a moment, it felt as though time had slowed, the weight of Sandy's illness pushed aside by the warmth of shared company.

As they began eating, John placed his fork down and cleared his throat. "Before we dig in, I think it's only right that we pray."

Everyone bowed their heads as John spoke, his voice steady and sincere. "Heavenly Father, we thank You for this meal, for the hands that prepared it, and for the blessing of this community. We ask for Your strength and guidance as we navigate the days ahead. Please watch over Sandy and bring her comfort. In Jesus' name, Amen."

"Amen," everyone echoed softly, lifting their heads.

Dr. Abbott recounted a humorous story from his residency days, earning a laugh from Sandy. Pastor Terry followed with a fond memory of a church picnic years ago, when Mae, as a teenager, had accidentally spilled lemonade all over the front of the mayor's pants.

"Oh, I remember that!" Sandy said, her voice light with laughter. "Mae turned so red, I thought she'd catch fire."

Mae groaned, though she couldn't suppress her grin. "I was mortified. I'm pretty sure the mayor avoided me for the rest of the summer."

"It was an honest mistake," Dara said, patting Mae's hand. "And besides, it gave us all a story to tell."

Pastor Terry's smile turned nostalgic. "Mae, do you remember the summer when you sang the lead in the choir at church camp?"

Mae froze mid-bite and groaned. "Oh no, not that story."

"Oh yes, that story," Dara said, laughing. "You were so nervous you almost backed out during rehearsal. But then, during the evening service, you stood up in front of everyone and sang your heart out. There wasn't a dry eye in the room."

She remembered that night at church camp vividly—how alive she had felt, how close to something bigger. And now? That girl felt like a stranger. Somewhere between job promotions and late nights in Midtown, she had misplaced her faith like an old sweater packed in a forgotten box.

Pastor Terry nodded, his expression warm. "That was the first time I realized how much potential you had, Mae—not just as a singer, but as someone who could inspire others. You were always a leader in the youth group."

Mae smiled despite herself, the memory pulling her back to those summers at church camp. She could still hear the sound of worship songs floating over the campfire, the way the stars seemed to shine brighter there. Church camp had been a place of joy, connection, and discovery, and it was under Pastor Terry and Dara's guidance that her faith had truly begun to blossom.

Dara's voice softened. "And don't forget the Bible study sessions we had. You always asked the best questions, Mae. Deep ones, the kind that made us all think a little harder about our beliefs."

Sandy, listening from her bed, chimed in. "Mae's always been philosophical, contemplative like that. She gets that from her father."

John chuckled quietly. "I don't know about that, but I do remember her coming home from church camp every year on fire for the Lord. She'd tell us every detail about the sermons, the activities, even the team games."

Mae laughed. "The team games were the best. But those campfire worship nights—that's what always stuck with me. It felt so real, so... personal."

As they spoke, Mae felt a pang of regret. When she had first moved to New York, she had been so focused on building her career that her faith had taken a back seat. Sundays had become just another workday or an opportunity to catch up on errands. Without a church community to anchor her, her connection to God had faded into the background of her life. She still prayed occasionally, especially during tough times, but it wasn't the same. She had always carried a low hum of guilt over it, but tonight, surrounded by the faith-driven kindness of her parents and their community, she felt something shift.

Mae's thoughts turned to Pastor Terry's earlier words: *God's been with you, even when you've been too busy to notice.*

She glanced at her mother's serene face as Sandy quoted her favorite verse: *"For I know the plans I have for you," declares the Lord. "Plans to prosper you and not to harm you, plans to give you hope and a future."* It was from **Jeremiah 29:11**, a promise Sandy had clung to through every storm. Her mother's faith, unwavering even now, was a living testament to the power of belief.

The words washed over her like warm light, so familiar they tugged at a thread woven into the fabric of who she was. Her mother had whispered that verse to her before every major moment in her life—her first basketball game, college move-in day, even the morning she boarded her first flight to New York. Hearing it now, at the edge of loss, it hit differently. Not as a promise of things to come—but as a call to return to what mattered.

As the meal wound down, Dara placed her hand on Mae's arm. "The congregation is organizing a meal train for you all. We'll make sure there's food here every evening, and if you need help with anything—chores, errands, anything—just say the word."

Mae blinked, her heart swelling at the kindness. "Thank you. That means so much."

After clearing plates, Pastor Terry stood and bowed his head. "Let's pray before we go." His voice was calm but resonant as he asked for strength, peace, and comfort for Sandy and her family. Mae closed her eyes, letting the prayer wash over her. It was the first time in years that she'd felt a connection to something larger than herself.

When Pastor Terry, Dara, and Dr. Abbott left, Mae and her dad walked them to the door, offering their heartfelt thanks.

The front door clicked shut behind their guests, and the house settled into a soft hush. Mae lingered by the entryway, her hand resting on the doorknob, not quite ready to move. Her father stood beside her, shoulders slightly slumped, eyes fixed on the quiet hallway.

They hadn't planned it—not exactly. But the timing had always been inevitable. Pastor Terry and Dara's visit had simply postponed the moment by a few precious hours. Now, with the evening quiet pressing in around them, there was nothing left in the way.

Mae looked up at her father, and he looked back. No words passed between them, but something moved in the silence—grief, resolve, fear. It was a shared under-standing, heavy and unspoken, the kind only family could carry together.

From down the hall came the steady hum of the oxygen machine, a low rhythm they had grown used to but never comfortable with.

Mae slipped her arm through her father's, and he let out a quiet breath, almost like a sigh. As they began walking, she leaned her head gently against his shoulder, just for a moment. It wasn't a gesture of weakness—it was one of love. Of strength borrowed and shared.

Side by side, they moved down the hallway, toward the room that held the truth neither of them wanted to speak—but both knew had to be heard.

Sandy rested back against the pillows, her eyes heavy-lidded but alert. John sat on the edge of the bed, silent, his hand wrapped around hers. Mae stood nearby, unsure if she should speak or wait for her father to.

Finally, Sandy looked between them and said softly, "You don't have to say it. I already know."

Mae's breath caught.

"I've known for a while now," Sandy continued, her voice like wind through leaves. "I just needed to hear it from you. So, I can stop pretending and start preparing."

John bowed his head, a tear slipping down his cheek. Mae reached for her mother's hand, and realized that maybe strength didn't always look like fighting. Some-times it looked like surrender. Graceful, quiet surrender.

Sandy took a slow breath, her gaze soft but clear. "I've always believed life is a story we get to write, chapter by chapter," she said, her fingers resting lightly on the edge of the quilt. "We don't always get to choose the ending, but we do get to decide what matters along the way."

Mae blinked back tears. Her throat tightened.

Sandy looked toward John, then back at Mae. "There's been heartbreak, sure. But also joy. Plenty of joy. And I wouldn't trade a single chapter of it."

The moment lingered in the quiet that followed, tender and weighty. Mae gave her mother's hand a final squeeze, then gently rose as Sandy drifted into a light sleep. She and her father stepped out of the room together, neither speaking.

In the hallway, Mae felt the familiar numbness begin to settle over her again, like fog rolling in over still water. The ache in her heart threatened to rise, but she forced it back down—back into the box she'd sealed in her mind, the one she didn't dare open just yet. This wasn't the time. Her dad needed her.

She glanced at him beside her, his face drawn and distant, his steps slow. She couldn't fall apart now—not while he was unraveling one thread at a time. So she swallowed her grief and steadied her breath, wrapping herself in a thin layer of control.

In the living room, they sat in silence, the day's emotions crackling softly between them like the static of an old record—imperfect, unrelenting, and achingly familiar.

"You okay, Dad?" Mae asked softly.

John nodded, leaning back against the cushions. "It's a lot, Mae. But we'll get through it. Together."

She studied him, noticing the exhaustion in his eyes, the way his shoulders carried the weight of the day. Yet his voice was steady, unwavering. The quiet strength she had always admired in him was still there, even now.

But as she watched him, Mae saw it—*the way he was doing exactly what she was.* Holding it in. Swallowing the grief. Trying to be the strong one.

She wondered, not without a touch of fear, *which one of them would break first.*

He paused, then glanced at her. "You're a lot like your mother, you know. Strong, steady, and full of grace. She's proud of you. And so am I."

Mae swallowed the lump rising in her throat, managing a small smile. "Thanks, Dad."

John squeezed her hand gently, his calloused palm warm against hers. "Now, get some rest. Tomorrow's another day."

"Goodnight, Dad," Mae said, rising slowly. She turned toward the stairs, but not before casting one last glance back at him—wondering if he, too, was waiting until the house went still before letting go.

Upstairs, Mae stepped into her old bedroom. It was just as she had left it—soft pastel walls, shelves lined with books and basketball trophies, and her old quilt folded neatly at the foot of the bed. The scent of lavender and aged paper lingered in the air, a familiar comfort. She ran her fingers over the quilt, memories of Sunday mornings, church picnics, and her mother's hymns flooding back.

She sank onto the mattress, the springs creaking slightly beneath her weight. The night was still, save for the rhythmic chirp of crickets outside her window. Sliding beneath the quilt, she let out a slow breath, staring at the ceiling.

Prayer wasn't something she turned to anymore, and yet, she whispered a tentative prayer: *God, I don't know what I'm doing, but I need help. Please guide me.*

It felt strange, almost foreign, as if the words were stretching muscles she hadn't used in years. But as she lay there in the stillness, something in her soul loosened.

A single tear slipped down her cheek. Then another. Silent and unforced.

She didn't sob. Didn't break. But the tears came anyway—soft and slow, trickling across her temples and into her hairline. It wasn't grief, exactly. Not fear. Just a release. A quiet surrender.

As she closed her eyes, a flicker of peace settled in—fragile but present. Her mother's words from earlier echoed in her mind: *Sometimes, the things we leave behind are the things we're meant to come back to.*

Mae let the words settle in her heart as she drifted off to sleep.

# Chapter 9

# Introductions

The next morning, Mae woke up feeling something she hadn't experienced in a while—relief. Relief wasn't the same as peace, but it was enough to get her out of bed without feeling like the air was too heavy to breathe. Her mind felt clearer, her body lighter, as though the weight of the past two days had momentarily lifted. The golden morning sun poured through the curtains, bathing her childhood room in warmth. She stretched, glancing at the clock, surprised to see it was already 9 a.m. Sleeping in wasn't something she allowed herself often, but today, it felt like a small victory.

As she descended the stairs, the rich aroma of freshly brewed coffee greeted her. In the living room, her father sat in his favorite armchair, his Bible open on his lap. His elbow rested on one knee, his thumb idly flipping through the pages. Mae knew this ritual well—it was his way of seeking strength, of finding clarity in the face of uncertainty. She'd seen him sit like this her whole life—steady, centered—but now she noticed the fatigue at the corners of his eyes. The kind of tired that sleep wouldn't fix.

"Morning, Dad," Mae said, her voice still thick with sleep.

Her father looked up and smiled. "Morning, sweetheart. Sleep well?"

"Better than I have in ages," she admitted, heading toward the kitchen. She poured herself a mug of coffee, inhaling the deep, bitter aroma. One sip confirmed what she already knew—her dad's preference for Folgers wasn't doing her any favors. With a slight grimace, she added an extra spoonful of sugar and a generous dose of cream, determined to make it drinkable.

As she returned to the living room, she noticed her dad studying his Bible intently. "Looking for something in particular?" she asked, settling onto the couch.

He nodded, his expression thoughtful. "Just needed a little encouragement this morning. Dr. Abbott called earlier—he's stopping by later and bringing someone with him to introduce to us."

Mae arched a brow. "Someone? Who?"

Her father shrugged. "Didn't say much, just that it's someone who'll be helping us out."

Mae raised an eyebrow, her grip tightening slightly on her coffee mug. She didn't like unknowns—especially now, when everything felt fragile.

Mae took another sip of her coffee, filing the information away for later. "Have you eaten yet?"

Her dad shook his head. "Not yet. I was waiting for you."

Mae smiled, standing and gesturing toward the kitchen. "Well, come on. Let's make something."

They moved around the kitchen in easy rhythm—cracking eggs, buttering toast, the sizzle of the skillet filling the quiet. It wasn't just breakfast. It was a ritual, a way of reclaiming something steady in a world that had begun to tilt. "You think Mom's up for breakfast with us?" Mae asked as she mashed a banana to mix into the pancake batter.

"I think so," her dad replied. "She loves your banana pancakes—especially with that huckleberry syrup."

Mae smiled, remembering how her mother would always light up at the sight of her favorite breakfast. They plated the food and carried it upstairs together.

Sandy was already awake, sitting up in bed and brushing her hair. Despite the pallor in her cheeks, there was a brightness in her eyes that made Mae feel a surge of hope. "Good morning, Mom," Mae said, setting the tray on the nightstand.

Sandy's face lit up when she saw the pancakes. "You didn't!"

"Banana pancakes with huckleberry syrup," Mae said, grinning. "You deserve a treat."

The three of them ate together, the sound of clinking forks and soft laughter filling the room. They reminisced about old times, their voices growing more animated as the memories poured out.

"You remember that time Jim Carter drove Mae home from school?" Sandy asked, her eyes twinkling.

Mae froze, her fork halfway to her mouth. "Oh, no. Don't tell this story."

Her dad chuckled. "I had to stay late after practice to help some of the boys with conditioning, if I recall. Jim offered to give you a ride. Seemed harmless enough."

Sandy laughed. "Harmless? I overheard you later that night on the phone with your girlfriends, Mae. You were practically bragging about how the star quarterback drove you home."

Mae's cheeks burned. "I did not!"

"Oh, you did," her mom teased, taking another bite of pancake. "You had stars in your eyes for days."

Mae shook her head, embarrassed but smiling despite herself. She had forgotten about that moment. Now, though, it stirred something bittersweet—a reminder of the innocent crush she'd once had on Jim, long before life grew complicated.

After breakfast, Sandy insisted on taking a shower to freshen up. Though she was weak, her determination to maintain a sense of normalcy comforted Mae. It reminded her that there was still time—still moments to share, still memories to make.

Mae and her father returned to the kitchen, cleaning up the dishes together. As they worked, her dad's calm demeanor seemed to envelop the room.

"You know," he said, his voice steady, "your mom and I have had so many good years together. I try to focus on that—the good times. It helps."

Mae glanced at him, her hands paused over the sink. "How do you do it? Stay so... steady?"

Her father smiled faintly, rinsing a plate. "Faith, sweetheart. I've learned to rely on God for strength and wisdom. It's not always easy, but it's what gets me through. And it'll get you through, too."

His words settled deep in Mae's heart, a quiet reminder of the foundation her parents had always built their lives upon.

The doorbell rang just as they finished tidying up. Mae wiped her hands on a dish towel and headed to answer it. When she opened the door, she froze for a half beat.

Standing on the porch was a stunning woman in her late thirties, dressed in a tailored navy blouse tucked neatly into cream slacks, the kind that looked effortless but screamed expensive. Her blonde hair was styled in soft, polished waves that framed her face just so, and a delicate gold necklace rested at her collarbone, catching the morning light. Crystal-blue eyes sparkled beneath long lashes, and her bright, practiced smile radiated the kind of confidence Mae knew well—*too* well.

There was something familiar in the tilt of her head, the way she held her posture like she'd been trained to take up space without apology. Mae couldn't quite place it, but a flicker of recognition stirred beneath the surface, just out of reach.

"Hi there," the woman said, her voice chipper and melodic. "You must be Mae."

Mae blinked, caught slightly off guard. "Yes. And you are?"

Before the woman could respond, Dr. Abbott appeared behind her, stepping into view. "Mae, this is Crystal Morgan," he said warmly. "She's a hospice nurse—and an alumna of Twinsdale High. She'll be helping your family. You two know each other, don't you?"

And just like that, the flicker sparked into flame. Mae's stomach tightened. Of course. Crystal Morgan. The name alone unearthed a dozen half-buried memories—cheerleading uniforms, cafeteria whispers, and hallway glances with too much meaning.

"Of course," she said, forcing a polite smile. "Come in."

As Crystal stepped inside, her eyes flicked over Mae with subtle curiosity before scanning the house. "It's lovely here," she said lightly. "I'm so sorry to meet again under these circumstances."

"Thank you," Mae replied, her tone clipped but polite.

Crystal turned her attention to Dr. Abbott and John—whom she still referred to as Coach Whitaker—with a warm and polished ease. "It's truly an honor to be here," she said, her voice smooth and confident. "I know how much this family means to the community, and I'll do everything I can to make things easier during this time."

Mae stood slightly apart, arms loosely crossed, observing from the sidelines. She tried to stay present, to focus on what was happening now, but her mind churned with old memories. No amount of professional charm could erase the past.

Back in high school, Crystal had been the queen of manipulation—popular, poised, and always in control of the narrative. And when it came to Jim, she had wielded that power like a weapon. He had adored her, blind to the way she treated him as an accessory, a prop in the life she was meticulously crafting for herself. Mae had seen it all firsthand, but one memory burned sharper than the rest: Crystal in the parking lot after a home football game, leaning too close to Gary Hopkins, her laughter drifting through the night. Mae had wanted to tell Jim, to warn him, but she hadn't known how. And then, just months later, Crystal had delivered the final blow—dumping Jim in front of nearly the entire senior class at the end-of-summer bonfire, like it was all part of some grand performance.

Then, she was gone. Off to Austin. Her family followed soon after, and Crystal had all but vanished from Twinsdale's memory. Until now.

Crystal turned her gaze to Mae, her professional smile softening, though Mae swore she caught a flicker of hesitation. "Mae," she said, her voice warm, practiced. "I know this is a difficult time, but I'm here to help however I can. We'll make this as comfortable as possible for your mom."

Mae, again, forced a polite smile. "Thank you. We appreciate that."

On the surface, Crystal appeared transformed—capable, composed, and, dare Mae say, kind. But could someone change that much? Or was this just another carefully constructed façade? Mae knew she should be focusing on her mother's care, not on over a decade-old grudge, but the unease coiling in her gut wouldn't go away.

Her father's voice cut through her thoughts. "Thank you for coming, Crystal," he said, his tone steady, kind. "We've heard great things about your work, and we're grateful to have you with us."

Crystal smiled graciously. "It's truly my honor, Coach. You made such an impact on my life, and I'm glad I can give back in some way."

"John," he corrected gently. "Call me John, please."

He glanced at Mae, then added, "When I spoke to Dr. Abbott earlier this morning, he suggested Crystal stay here in the guest room for the time being—said it would make things easier with the round-the-clock care. I told him it made sense. I hope that's okay."

Mae's polite smile didn't waver, but a ripple of unease moved through her chest. "Of course," she said smoothly. "Whatever makes things easier."

But inside, her thoughts tangled. She didn't like how fast this was happening—how Crystal already seemed to fit, already knew which words to say, already had her father's trust. Maybe it was fine. Maybe it was even helpful. But still, something about it didn't sit right.

She clenched her jaw at Crystal's words, but held her tongue. Whether this was genuine or just another performance, only time would tell. For now, there were more pressing matters.

She followed the group upstairs, watching as Crystal was introduced to her mother, listening as they discussed the plan for Sandy's care. But the unease lingered, settling into her bones like a storm on the horizon, just waiting to break.

Two days passed in a haze of whispered updates and pill reminders. Crystal had taken over the guest room without missing a beat and, somehow, had also taken over the house it seemed. She moved with unearned ease, knowing where to find extra blankets, how to load the dishwasher without asking, even which drawers held the heating pads.

Mae didn't know whether to be grateful or irritated. Probably both. On the one hand, Crystal was competent, almost annoyingly so. On the other, she had this way of narrating her care as if Mae weren't right there.

"I found the extra linens in the hall closet," she'd say, folding neatly stacked towels with clinical precision. Or, "I noticed Sandy's appetite dipped a bit yesterday, so I adjusted the schedule slightly." Always polite, always efficient, always speaking in careful half-smiles and gentle tones that didn't match the Crystal Mae remembered.

Mae kept catching herself studying her mother's face too long—watching the way her jaw stayed slack now when she slept, or how she paused before answering, like words took longer to rise to the surface. Sandy was still lucid, still herself—but thinner. Softer around the edges. Like someone fading out of a photograph.

Mae told herself she wasn't keeping score. That it didn't matter who fluffed the pillows first or who tracked the medication times more precisely. But then Crystal would say something like, "Did you notice she's breathing shallower today?" and Mae would feel her stomach twist in guilt.

Mae wasn't sure if she was exhausted or just unraveling slowly, thread by thread. Everything felt too quiet, too managed—like the silence before something gave way.

Something was coming. She could feel it. She just didn't know if it would come from Sandy, Crystal, or herself.

# Chapter 10

# Building Trust

Whatever Mae had been waiting for, it wasn't this.

Not the efficiency. Not the gentleness. Not the surreal feeling of being the least steady person in the room.

Mae kept her arms crossed as she watched Crystal work, standing just close enough to observe but far enough to keep a wall between them. Crystal, to her credit, seemed unfazed by Mae's silent scrutiny. She moved through the room with a quiet efficiency, adjusting Sandy's pillows, smoothing out the blanket, and checking the oxygen levels with practiced ease. Her every action was measured, careful, reassuring.

Sandy stirred slightly, shifting against the pillows with a wince. Crystal immediately noticed. "Let's try adjusting you a little, Sandy," she said, her voice gentle as she helped ease Sandy into a more comfortable position. "There we go. How's that?"

Sandy exhaled slowly, nodding. "Better," she admitted, though her voice was thinner than Mae remembered. "Sitting up helps."

Crystal reached for the glass of water on the nightstand, adding a straw before offering it to Sandy. "Try a few sips. Small ones. We want to keep you feeling strong."

Sandy took a sip, her tired eyes flickering open to meet Crystal's. "You're good at this," she murmured, the gratitude clear in her voice.

Crystal smiled, her expression softening. "I had a great mentor when I first started nursing. She always said care should feel like kindness."

Mae remained quiet, watching the interaction with an uneasy mix of skepticism and reluctant admiration. She wasn't ready to let her guard down—not yet—but she couldn't deny that Crystal was competent, even warm, in a way Mae hadn't expected.

Still, the past clung to her.

The girl she remembered from high school wasn't kind. She was calculated. Crystal had been the queen bee—charming to adults, cutting to anyone who didn't serve her image. Mae had seen it all: how she used Jim like a status symbol, how she dismissed others who didn't fit her mold, how quickly she turned cruel when attention drifted from her spotlight. Mae had carried that memory with her for years—especially the way Crystal humiliated Jim at the end-of-summer bonfire. It wasn't just teenage drama. It was callous. Public.

But that was a lifetime ago.

Mae sighed quietly, her arms still folded across her chest. High school girls could be awful—herself included, if she was honest. People weren't supposed to be held to the worst versions of who they used to be. Not forever.

She glanced at Crystal again, who was now adjusting the bedside table with practiced ease, unaware of the storm of memories brewing just a few feet away.

*Maybe people really do change.*

The thought didn't come easily, but it settled inside her like a loose thread waiting to be pulled.

As the afternoon wore on, Crystal and Mae settled into a quiet rhythm, tending to Sandy's needs together. When Mae wasn't fetching water or adjusting blankets, she listened to the steady, calming tone Crystal used when speaking to her mother. There was no impatience, no strain, only understanding. And Mae could see that Sandy responded to it, her body relaxing slightly, her breathing easier.

Later that evening, after Sandy had fallen asleep, Mae followed Crystal into the kitchen. The air was thick with the smell of chamomile tea, something her father had started making every night to help Sandy rest. Crystal leaned against the counter, rolling her shoulders as though working out tension.

"I wasn't sure what to expect from you," Mae admitted, crossing her arms. "But I have to say, you know what you're doing."

Crystal arched a brow, a wry smile playing at her lips. "I'll take that as a compliment."

Mae exhaled, glancing toward the darkened hallway where her mother's bedroom was. "She likes you. That matters."

Crystal studied her for a long moment, something unreadable flickering in her gaze. "I get it, Mae. You remember who I was, not who I am. And that's fair.

But I promise you this—I'm here to help. For your mom. And for your family. That's what matters to me now."

Mae lifted the teapot and poured herself a cup, watching the steam curl from the rim. She let Crystal's words settle, turning them over in her mind before replying, her voice quieter now. "I guess that's all that really matters."

Crystal's smile didn't falter, but something in her eyes shifted—acknowledgment, maybe even under-standing. And for tonight, at least, the wall between them felt a little less solid.

The next morning, Mae woke to the scent of fresh coffee drifting through the house, mingling with the soft hush of conversation down the hall. Sunlight streamed through her bedroom window, casting a golden glow over the quilt at the foot of her bed. She blinked awake, surprised to find her body still, her breath even. No racing pulse, no tight chest. Just... morning.

Stretching, she swung her legs over the side of the bed and listened. Her mother's voice, though weaker than usual, carried through the house in quiet conver-sation. She wasn't alone—Crystal was with her, tending to her needs with a gentle efficiency.

Mae stepped into the hallway bathroom, the chill of the tile waking her a little more. She brushed her teeth in silence, the hum of the electric toothbrush the only sound in the early morning stillness. After rinsing, she leaned over the sink and splashed cold water on her face, letting it chase away the last traces of sleep. Her reflection stared back at her—tired, yes, but steadier than she'd been days ago.

Freshened up, Mae padded down the hall, pausing at the doorway to her mother's room. There she saw Crystal sitting beside Sandy, holding her Bible in her lap. Crystal looked up as Mae entered, offering a small smile.

"Perfect timing! Your mom just asked me to read to her," Crystal said gently, closing the Bible. "But I think she'd prefer to hear it from you."

Mae blinked, taken slightly off guard by the gesture. Sandy's eyes flickered to her daughter, warm with affection.

"Would you, sweetheart?" Sandy asked.

Mae nodded, stepping forward as Crystal stood.

"I'll go grab a quick shower while you two have some time," Crystal offered, placing the Bible gently in Mae's hands. "Let me know if either of you need anything."

"Thank you," Mae said, polite but cool.

Crystal gave a small nod and slipped out of the room, the sound of her footsteps fading down the hallway.

Mae held the Bible, her fingers brushing the worn leather cover. It was a simple moment, but one that wasn't lost on her. Crystal could have stayed. Could have read. But instead, she had chosen to step aside, allowing Mae and her mother to share something sacred between them.

Sandy's gaze lingered on Mae. "You're holding back," she said softly. "Not with me. With her."

Mae gave a tight shrug, eyes still on the Bible. "She wasn't always so... thoughtful."

Sandy tilted her head slightly. "High school?"

Mae gave a faint nod. "She wasn't kind. Not to me. Not to a lot of people. Especially not to Jim." She hesitated, then added, "I know people change. I just—don't trust it yet."

Sandy reached for her daughter's hand, her fingers thin but still steady. "What we choose to dwell on," she murmured, "shapes who we become. You can't always control what happens. But you can choose what to carry with you."

Mae didn't answer right away. Her mother's words hung in the air, soft but weighty, like a stone dropped into water. *What you choose to carry.* It echoed in her mind's eye, nudging something that had been tightly held. She wasn't ready to let go of the past—not completely—but maybe, just maybe, she could stop gripping it so hard.

Sandy smiled faintly, resting her head against the pillow. "Now, how about that reading?"

Mae held the Bible, her fingers brushing the worn leather cover. "Of course, Mom. What passage?"

Sandy's voice was barely above a whisper. "I like to just open it up and read wherever my finger lands."

Mae nodded, letting the pages fan beneath her fingertips before allowing them to settle. She pressed her finger gently onto the thin paper and glanced down at the words beneath it. Her breath caught slightly when she saw where she had landed—**Isaiah 40:28–31**.

Clearing her throat softly, she began to read:

**"Do you not know? Have you not heard?**

The Lord is the everlasting God,
the Creator of the ends of the earth.
He will not grow tired or weary,
and his understanding no one can fathom.
He gives strength to the weary
and increases the power of the weak.
Even youths grow tired and weary,
and young men stumble and fall;
but those who hope in the Lord
will renew their strength.
They will soar on wings like eagles;
they will run and not grow weary,
they will walk and not be faint."

Mae's voice remained steady, but the meaning behind the words settled deep within her. She glanced up, finding Sandy watching her with soft eyes, her expression peaceful.

"That's always been one of my favorites," Sandy murmured.

Mae reached for her mother's hand, giving it a light squeeze. "Mine too."

Sandy shifted slightly beneath the quilt, then patted the empty space beside her. "Come here, baby," she said, her voice barely above a whisper.

Mae hesitated for only a moment before slipping off the chair and carefully easing onto the bed beside her mother, curling into the familiar space as she had so many times as a child. Sandy's arm wrapped around her, frail but steady, and her fingers gently began to comb through Mae's hair in slow, rhythmic strokes.

The touch—light, soothing—sent a warmth through Mae's body, softening the tension she didn't realize she'd still been holding. Sandy hummed a lullaby under her breath, the same one she used to sing when Mae was small and scared of thunderstorms. The sound was low, tender, and achingly familiar.

For a few moments, they lay together in silence, the words and melody lingering in the air like a blessing. Eventually, Sandy's breathing deepened, her body relaxing as sleep took over.

The sound of the door easing open pulled Mae from her thoughts. Crystal stood there, her voice hushed. "She looks comfortable."

Mae nodded. "She is."

Crystal stepped forward, her expression calm. "I'll stay with her if you want to take some time with your dad. He mentioned he could use some help around the house."

Mae hesitated, torn between staying and the quiet understanding that Crystal was offering her something valuable—time.

"She'll be okay," Crystal reassured. "And if she needs anything, I'll be right here."

Mae studied her for a moment, then exhaled. "Thanks."

Crystal only nodded, settling into the chair beside Sandy's bed as Mae quietly slipped out of the room.

As she made her way downstairs, she realized something had shifted. It wasn't trust, not yet—but it was something close. And for now, that was enough.

Mae found her father outside on the back porch, sitting on the old wooden bench swing, his hands wrapped around a steaming cup of coffee. The morning sun cast long shadows across the yard, the dew still fresh on the blades of grass. It was a beautiful day—one that felt almost at odds with the heaviness pressing on their family.

He looked up as Mae stepped outside, offering a small smile. "Your mother asleep?"

Mae nodded, settling beside him on the swing. "Yeah, Crystal's sitting with her. She suggested I come spend some time with you."

John exhaled slowly, nodding in quiet appreciation. He took a sip of his coffee before setting the cup down on the armrest. "I don't know what we would do without the people around us. The way everyone has stepped up... it's humbling."

Mae folded her hands in her lap, watching as a soft breeze rustled the trees. "Dad... how are you really doing?" she asked, turning to face him. "I know you're being strong for Mom and for me, but... you don't have to carry all of this alone."

Her father was silent for a long moment, staring out over the pasture beyond their backyard. When he finally spoke, his voice was thick with emotion. "I knew this day would come eventually," he admitted. "I just thought we'd have more time. Your mother... she's always been the heart of this home. I don't know how to picture this place without her."

Mae swallowed hard, reaching for his hand. "I can't either."

John squeezed her hand gently, his grip warm and familiar. "But I do know one thing," he said, his voice growing steadier. "Your mother wouldn't want us to fall apart. She's made this house a home, and when the time comes, we'll carry that forward. We'll keep her here with us, in the way we live, in the way we love each other. That's how we honor her."

Mae blinked rapidly, pushing back the sting of tears. "You always know what to say."

He let out a quiet chuckle. "Not always. But I do know that when you love someone the way I love your mother, you don't let grief steal the good. We'll be sad, we'll hurt, but we'll also remember her with joy."

Mae nodded, leaning her head against his shoulder, seeking the comfort she hadn't even realized she needed. "I love you, Dad."

"I love you too, sweetheart." He kissed the top of her head, letting his arm rest around her shoulders. "And I promise you, we'll get through this. Together."

They sat there for a long time, watching the world wake up around them, drawing strength from each other in the quiet morning light.

The rest of the morning slipped away into a steady rhythm of movement and purpose. Mae threw herself into helping her father with chores, grateful for the distraction and the sense of usefulness it brought. Together, they dusted off forgotten corners of the house, sorted through stacks of mail that had accumulated on the kitchen counter, and even took a moment to fix the loose hinge on the back door—something John had been meaning to get to for weeks.

"You know, I could get used to having an extra set of hands around here," John said, giving Mae an appreciative glance as she carried a fresh basket of laundry to the bedroom.

Mae smirked over her shoulder. "Don't get too comfortable. I still have a life back in New York."

Her father chuckled but didn't respond, and Mae let the words hang in the air. Even as she said them, she wasn't sure how true they felt anymore.

By noon, they turned their attention to preparing lunch for Sandy. John took the lead on grilling up simple turkey and cheese sandwiches while Mae sliced fresh fruit and poured iced tea. The aroma of toasted bread and melted cheese filled the kitchen, mingling with the faint scent of the wild bluebonnets that had sprouted unexpectedly along the fence line in the yard.

When Mae pointed them out through the kitchen window, her father smiled, his gaze going soft with memory.

"They were always her favorite," he murmured. "Every spring, she'd say she wanted to go driving just to see the fields of them stretching for miles. Said it made her feel like Texas was hugging her back."

Mae swallowed the lump in her throat, nodding. "They showed up just in time, then."

On a quiet impulse, Mae slipped out the back door and walked along the fence, carefully picking a small handful of the delicate blossoms. Their vibrant blue petals shimmered in the sunlight, and she cupped them gently in her hand like something sacred. When she returned to the kitchen, she arranged the flowers on the edge of Sandy's lunch plate—a soft splash of color, a whisper of spring.

John caught her eye, his expression warm. "She'll love that."

Together, they carried the tray upstairs, John holding the iced tea while Mae balanced the plate. When they stepped into Sandy's room, they were met with the soft hum of conversation. Crystal sat at the bedside, adjusting Sandy's pillows with practiced care, her voice gentle as she spoke.

"I've been told I make a mean cup of chamomile tea," Crystal was saying. "Maybe later, we can try some if you're up for it."

Sandy gave a tired smile. "That sounds lovely."

Mae stepped forward with the tray. "Lunch is ready, Mom," she said, setting it gently on the nightstand.

Crystal stepped back smoothly, giving Mae space. "I'll let you three enjoy some time together. I'll be downstairs if you need me."

Mae hesitated, watching Crystal for a moment longer before nodding. "Thanks, Crystal."

Crystal returned the nod with a small, knowing smile before slipping out of the room.

Sandy glanced down at the tray, her gaze catching on the bluebonnets. Her eyes softened, shining with sudden emotion. "Oh, Mae... you remembered."

Mae smiled and sat beside her. "They're blooming along the fence line. Couldn't resist."

John pulled up a chair on Sandy's other side, carefully placing the iced tea within her reach. "We thought you could use a little spring with your sandwich," he said, his voice quiet but warm.

Sandy reached for Mae's hand and gave it a gentle squeeze. "They're beautiful. Just like you."

The three of them ate together in companionable quiet, the kind that didn't need filling. Every now and then, John would adjust Sandy's straw or add a wedge of fruit to her plate, and Mae would brush a crumb from her mother's lap, or refill her glass. It was simple, intimate—more than a meal. It was a moment of stillness in the middle of the storm, a quiet pause where love spoke louder than words, and presence was the only thing that mattered.

As Mae sat with them, watching her mother take a careful bite of sandwich, she realized she wasn't just tolerating Crystal's presence—she was beginning to appreciate it. Not fully. Not without hesitation. But the edges of resentment had softened, if only slightly, worn down by quiet gestures and unexpected kindness.

After lunch, Mae had stayed upstairs while Sandy drifted off to sleep, tidying the room and quietly sorting through laundry while her father headed out to run a few errands. When the doorbell rang downstairs, she barely registered it, too focused on easing her mother into a more comfortable position.

It wasn't until she came down an hour later that she noticed the trays on the counter and the scent of slow-smoked brisket in the air—sweet and savory, unmistakably familiar.

Her dad beamed when she entered the kitchen. "Jim Carter himself," he said, gesturing to the spread like a proud host. "Brought half the menu from Rocket Ribs. Best dinner we've had in a while."

Mae's hands stilled on the dish towel she'd been folding. Jim had been here. Just downstairs. While she was upstairs, completely unaware.

She nodded slowly, trying to mask the knot tighten-ing in her stomach. "Oh."

"You missed him," Crystal said casually from across the kitchen, unwrapping a tray of cornbread. "I told him you were with your mom. He understood."

Mae forced a nod, brushing a strand of hair behind her ear. "That's good."

Crystal seemed lighter than usual, her movements unhurried as she stirred a spoon through a pot of baked beans. There was something easy in the way she moved, like she was still carrying the energy of a pleasant interaction.

"Jim's always been thoughtful," she added, almost offhandedly. "We had a nice chat, actually."

Mae's fingers tightened slightly around the edge of the counter. "Oh?"

Crystal glanced up, her expression unreadable—but something in the deliberate softness of her voice made Mae's skin prickle. "Yeah. It's been a while since we really talked, but it was nice. He's done well for himself."

Mae busied herself with the place settings, keeping her expression neutral. Jim's life was his own. And she had more important things to focus on—like caring for her mother, keeping her father grounded, and managing the emotional minefield of this house.

Still, as she sat down for dinner, the scent of brisket and barbecue sauce lingering in the air, her appetite wasn't what it had been a moment ago.

# Chapter 11

# A Breaking Point

The evening had settled quietly over the house, the soft hum of crickets outside blending with the rhythmic ticking of the kitchen clock. Mae stood at the sink, rinsing a washcloth, the warm water running over her fingers as she wrung it out. Behind her, Crystal wiped down the counters, her movements slower than usual, almost hesitant.

Sandy had finally drifted off to sleep after a long day, and with the house quiet, there was a moment of stillness that felt heavier than usual. Mae had grown accustomed to these late-night moments—working in sync with Crystal to tidy up, their words minimal, their focus the same. Tonight, though, something felt different.

As they worked side by side in the kitchen, the evening air settled around them, warm and thick with the scent of dish soap and the faintest trace of barbecue that still lingered from dinner. The soft hum of cicadas filtered in through the open window, and for a while, the only sounds between them were the clink of dishes and the steady rhythm of running water.

Crystal rinsed the last plate and set it in the drying rack before drying her hands on a dish towel. She hesitated for a moment, as if debating something, before finally speaking.

"I wasn't sure if I should say this," she began, her voice softer than usual. "But seeing Jim today... it made me realize something."

Mae stilled, her grip tightening on the washcloth she had been wringing out. She kept her expression neutral, her movements deliberate as she set the cloth aside and turned slightly toward Crystal. "Oh?"

Crystal let out a quiet, almost self-conscious laugh. "I didn't realize how much I missed him until I saw him again. It was like no time had passed since high school, but at the same time, everything was different. High school

Crystal should've come with a warning label. I was all attitude, hair spray, and way too much eyeliner. How anyone put up with me, I'll never know."

"He looks good, doesn't he?" She smiled, as if lost in a memory.

Mae forced a small nod. "Yeah. He does."

"I don't know why I'm telling you all this," she added, her voice quieter now. "I think I just needed to say it out loud—to hear myself work through it."

She glanced down at the dish towel in her hands, her fingers fidgeting with the hem.

"I know we're not close or anything, but... I guess I could really use some advice."

She paused, then let out a small breath, her expression softening.

"The feelings I had after seeing him really caught me off guard, honestly. I didn't expect to feel anything after all this time."

Crystal leaned against the counter, crossing her arms. "When I heard he was back in Texas, I couldn't stop thinking about what we had. I guess part of me wondered if there was still something there—if maybe he felt it too."

She looked away, her voice quieter now. "That wasn't why I took this job... not officially, anyway. But I think maybe, deep down, I wanted a chance to see if anything was still there."

Mae kept her face carefully composed, focusing on drying a dish even though her hands had gone clammy. "And? Did you get that feeling from him?"

Crystal tilted her head, considering. "I think so," she admitted, a flicker of hope in her voice. "We talked for a while when he dropped off the food, and there were moments... I don't know, moments that made me think maybe we could have another chance. I know we didn't end things well before, but people change, right?"

Mae swallowed down the sudden tightness in her throat, her fingers gripping the dish towel a little too tightly. She nodded, her voice even. "Yeah. People can change."

Crystal exhaled, looking almost relieved. "I guess we'll see what happens. I mean, I'm not in a rush. But it was nice, talking to him again. It felt familiar, you know?"

Mae nodded again, offering a tight smile. "That's good. I hope it works out for you."

Crystal beamed. "Thanks, Mae."

Mae had braced herself for a performance. A polished, manipulative monologue. But what she got instead was... honesty. Or at least something close to it. And that unsettled her more than she cared to admit.

Mae gave a small nod, turning back to the sink to busy herself with another dish. But as she scrubbed, she couldn't shake the lingering weight in her chest, the quiet ache she didn't dare name.

Because whatever Crystal had felt in her conversation with Jim, Mae had no doubt she believed it was real. And maybe it was. But the thought of it settled in Mae's stomach like a stone, heavy and unshakable.

The phone rang, breaking the quiet rhythm of the kitchen as Mae wiped down the counter. She glanced at the screen, feeling a rush of relief when she saw Jenny's name flashing. This was the first time they'd actually talked since she arrived in Texas, even though they had been texting daily. Mae had kept Jenny updated—her mother's condition, her father's struggle to hold everything together, and of course, the unexpected reappearance of Jim and Crystal. But text messages were just words on a screen. This call felt different. More real.

"I need to take this," Mae said, her voice brisk as she stepped away from the sink. Crystal, who was still drying dishes, barely looked up. Mae pushed open the back door and stepped onto the porch, the cool night air wrapping around her as she pressed the phone to her ear. "Hey, Jenny."

"Hey yourself," Jenny's voice came through, light but laced with something knowing. "Took you long enough to actually call me."

Mae sighed, leaning against the railing. "Yeah. Sorry. Things have just been... a lot."

"I know," Jenny said, and for a moment, her voice softened. "You've been keeping me updated, but how are you? Really?"

Mae rubbed her forehead, exhaustion settling deep in her bones. "I don't even know where to start."

"Start with your mom. How's she doing?"

Mae exhaled, glancing back at the house. "She's tired. Weaker than she lets on. Some days are better than others, but... I can see it, Jen. It's happening."

Jenny was quiet for a second, then said, "I'm so sorry, Mae. I wish I could be there."

"I know," Mae murmured. "My dad... he's holding it together, but I can tell it's getting harder for him."

"You told me he's been leaning on you more," Jenny said. "That's a good thing. He needs you."

"Yeah," Mae agreed, staring out at the darkened hills beyond the yard. "It helps, having something to do. Keeping busy."

There was a beat of silence before Jenny's voice turned sly. "Speaking of keeping busy... how's avoiding Jim going?"

Mae let out a short laugh, but it lacked any real amusement. "I'm not avoiding him."

"Right," Jenny drawled. "That's why you've texted me, let's see, three different times about how you managed to dodge him."

Mae closed her eyes. She should have known Jenny would catch onto that. "It's complicated."

"Oh, I bet it is," Jenny said, her tone turning wry. "Especially with Crystal in the mix."

Mae hesitated. This was the part she hadn't told Jenny in detail yet. The past text messages had been brief: *Crystal's here. She's Mom's nurse.* And then later, *Did I mention Crystal used to date Jim?*

But now, Mae had to say it out loud.

"She told me," Mae admitted, gripping the railing a little tighter. "Crystal. She told me why she really took this job."

Jenny groaned. "Oh no. Please tell me it's not what I think it is."

Mae forced a laugh, though it felt hollow. "She said she wanted to see if there was still something between her and Jim. And she thinks... she thinks maybe he felt something too."

Mae traced the grain of the wooden railing with her thumb, the familiar tightness settling back in her chest. "It doesn't matter," she said after a moment. "If Jim wants to give her another chance, that's his decision. It's none of my business."

Jenny was quiet for a second before she said, "Mae, do you hear yourself? You sound like you're trying to convince yourself that you don't care."

Mae closed her eyes, inhaling deeply. "Jenny—"

"No, listen to me," Jenny cut in. "You can pretend all you want, but I know you. And I know that this is bothering you a whole lot more than you're letting on."

Mae opened her mouth, then closed it again. She didn't want to go down this road. Not now. Not when there were more important things to focus on. "I have to go," she said instead, her voice softer now. "I just... I just needed to get that off my chest."

Jenny sighed, but didn't push further. "Alright. But Mae?"

"Yeah?"

Jenny's voice was gentler now, but firm. "Just promise me something. Don't let her get in your head."

Mae hesitated, then nodded. "I'll try."

But as she hung up and stared out into the darkness, she knew it wouldn't be that easy.

Mae ended the call and slipped the phone into her pocket, Jenny's words still echoing in her ears. Don't let her get in your head. If only it were that simple. Her mind was already full—crowded with worry, with grief, with the ache of trying to be everything for everyone.

She stood for a moment on the back porch, the night air cool against her skin, before finally turning back inside. The house was still, dimly lit, humming with the quiet sounds of routine and illness. As Mae stepped into the kitchen, the scent of chamomile lingered—soft and comforting. And then she noticed something: there was no one else around. No one to check on. No one to comfort.

Just her. And the silence.

The silence settled around her like a weighted blanket. She stared at the steam curling from the mug, letting it blur her vision, willing it to distract her from the ache in her heart.

She had kept it together for days—had locked away the truth in a little box in her mind, sealed tight so she could function, so she could be strong. But now, in this quiet, no one was watching. No one needed her to smile or say the right thing. And the box... it started to rattle. Cracks spiderwebbed across its surface. The news, the grief, the looming loss she hadn't dared examine—suddenly, it all pressed against the edges.

Her throat burned. Her vision blurred. She blinked, blinked again, but the tears came anyway.

Mae set the mug down with trembling hands and stepped away from the counter. The kitchen suddenly felt too small, too bright. She slipped out the back door again, letting it close softly behind her, and sank onto the worn wooden steps of the porch.

The night pressed in around her—cool, quiet, and oblivious to the ache she could no longer hide. Crickets chirped in the darkness, their rhythm steady and indifferent. Mae pressed her palms to her face and let out a shaky breath, one that hitched in her chest and caught on something sharp. The tears came harder now, unrestrained and silent, slipping through her fingers as she leaned forward, elbows on her knees.

No one could see her here.

Not her father, trying to hold it together.

Not her mother, fading a little more each day.

Not the nurse down the hall or the doctor who'd tried to soften the truth.

Just Mae—and the pieces she hadn't dared feel until now.

She didn't wail. She didn't scream. But she broke, quietly, in the dark—just enough to breathe again.

She stayed like that for a while, folded in on herself, the silence wrapping around her as the weight she'd been carrying slowly bled out through her stillness.

When the tears finally stopped, she wiped her face with the back of her hand, straightened her spine, and drew in a deep breath.

The ache was still there, sharp and waiting, but she shoved the rest of it back into the box. It would hold—for now. Tomorrow was coming, wrapped in the soft cruelty of time running out.

# Chapter 12

# Misread Signs & Avoidance

Morning came quick after a restless night. Mae stepped into her mother's room, the soft whirring and rhythmic hum of the medical equipment filling the otherwise quiet space. Sandy was sound asleep, her breathing steady, her face serene. Mae lingered by the bedside, adjusting the blanket around her mother's shoulders, a small act of care in a situation where so much felt out of her hands. She let her fingers rest lightly on Sandy's, drawing comfort from the warmth of her skin.

"Love you, Mom," she whispered, even though Sandy couldn't hear her.

With a deep breath, Mae slipped out of the room, padding quietly down the hallway. The house felt still, save for the distant hum of medical equipment and the occasional creak of the wooden floorboards. The faint sound of her father working on the porch carried through the open window, the rhythmic scrape of sandpaper against wood filling the morning air. She found him standing by the railing, focused on smoothing out a section of worn trim, his brow furrowed in concentration.

"Morning, sweetheart," John greeted, glancing up as she stepped onto the porch. "Your mom's still asleep?"

Mae nodded, hugging her arms around herself against the lingering morning chill. "Yeah, she's resting. I just checked on her."

Her father set the sandpaper down and wiped his hands on a rag. "Crystal stepped out for a little bit. Said she'd be back soon."

Mae tried to keep her expression neutral. "Got it. I was actually thinking about going for a run."

John studied her for a moment, then gave a knowing nod. "Good idea. Might clear your head some."

She smiled faintly. "Maybe."

"I'll be here with your mom. Go on, get some fresh air."

Mae gave him a grateful look before heading back inside to grab her running shoes. She laced them up tighter than usual, as if the added pressure might somehow keep her thoughts from unraveling. Securing her headphones in place, she scrolled through her playlist until she found something steady, something driving. The moment she stepped outside, she hit play, letting the opening chords of **Florence + The Machine's** Dog Days Are Over pulse through her ears, the beat syncing with the anticipation bubbling in her heart. She exhaled sharply, stretched her legs, and then took off down the driveway, letting the music drown out everything else.

The crisp morning air greeted her as she set off down the familiar dirt road that led toward town. Her feet pounded against the gravel, matching the steady pulse of the song in her ears. But even as she ran, her thoughts refused to quiet. Crystal. Jim. The way Crystal had looked last night at the dinner table when Crystal casually mentioned seeing Jim earlier.

The scene played on a loop in Mae's mind, each word echoing louder with every step she took. Crystal's voice, casual yet deliberate, her eyes flickering with something Mae couldn't quite place. "I just wondered if maybe there was still something between us." Mae had forced a smile, nodded, even made some neutral remark about how nice that must have been. But she hadn't stopped thinking about it since. The idea of Crystal pursuing Jim had burrowed under her skin, lingering like an unanswered question. She had told herself it didn't matter—that Jim's life was his own—but the thought of them together...ugh.

So she ran.

By the time she reached the edge of Main Street, her breath was steady, her strides fluid. She slowed to a walk, tugging at the brim of her cap, letting her pulse settle. The scent of smoked meat drifted through the air, unmistakable and rich. Her eyes lifted to Rocket Ribs & BBQ just ahead, the familiar red-and-black sign standing tall against the morning sky.

She hesitated, debating whether to take a different route, but then she saw them.

Crystal stood on the restaurant's wide porch, laughing, her hand brushing Jim's arm in a way that felt too easy, too familiar. Jim, leaning against the railing, smirked at whatever she had said, though his posture remained relaxed, casual.

Mae's stomach twisted, but she yanked her gaze away before either of them could see her. She turned down the side street instead, picking up her pace.

Through her headphones, the steady beat of the first song began to fade, replaced by the opening chords of **Stronger** by Kelly Clarkson. The familiar anthem surged through her, the driving tempo syncing with her stride. The lyrics—about resilience, about moving forward—wrapped around her like armor, and Mae focused on the rhythm, willing the music to push away the thoughts she didn't want to entertain. She wasn't dwelling. She wasn't overthinking. She was just running.

What she hadn't noticed—what she couldn't hear—was Jim calling her name as she passed.

This was exactly why she avoided him. She had no claim on him, no right to feel the way she did, and yet just seeing them together stirred something deep. Something dangerous. Something she didn't want to examine too closely.

But as she put more distance between herself and the restaurant, another feeling crept in—guilt. Heavy and insistent. This wasn't what she should be thinking about. Not now. Not when her mother was slipping further away each day. Not when her father was doing everything he could to hold himself together.

She should be focused on them. On what mattered. Not on a man she had no business thinking about—and a woman who shouldn't even occupy space in her mind.

Her pace quickened, her breath coming harder. The music blasted in her ears, but it couldn't drown out the truth threading itself into her thoughts.

Mae slowed to a walk, her breaths sharp and uneven, the early evening air clinging to her skin. Her legs ached, but not as much as the thought she couldn't outrun.

She would've liked to imagine something with Jim—if life were different. If her mother weren't dying. If Crystal hadn't come back, all sincerity and open wounds. If Mae didn't have an entire life waiting in New York.

But those were too many ifs.

And Mae had never been one to chase maybes.

Whatever she felt—the flickers of warmth, the pull toward something familiar and good—wasn't enough to rewrite everything else. Right now, a relationship would be nothing but a distraction. A tempting one. But a distraction all the same.

She preferred clarity over chaos. Control over complication. She'd always believed that love was something you made space for—not something you stumbled into while your world was falling apart.

She leaned forward, hands on her knees, and let the ache settle in.

Mae returned home with her pulse still thrumming from the run. Her thoughts had quieted, her emotions tucked neatly back into the boxes where they belonged. The exercise hadn't cleared her mind exactly, but it had helped her find a kind of order. A sense of control.

She toed off her running shoes by the back door and grabbed a glass of water, the coolness steadying her.

This was what she needed—focus, discipline, clarity. No more letting her heart wander toward impossible things. No more entertaining ideas that didn't belong in her world right now.

She would put these foolish thoughts behind her. She was sure of it.

Or—at least, she told herself she was.

The house was quiet except for the steady hum of the medical equipment in her mother's room. After a quick shower, she dressed in a soft cotton tee and jeans, towel-drying her hair as she made her way down the hall. She lingered at her mother's doorway for a moment, listening to the rhythmic sound of her breathing, before stepping inside.

Sandy was awake, her head propped up on pillows, a book resting open on her lap. Her face lit up when she saw Mae. "There's my girl," she said, her voice warm, though laced with the inevitable fatigue that had settled deeper in recent days.

Mae smiled, walking over to sit at the edge of the bed. "Hey, Mom. How are you feeling?"

"Better now that you're here," Sandy teased, reaching for Mae's hand. "Tell me about your run. Did you see anything interesting?"

Mae hesitated for a fraction of a second before forcing an easy nod. "Just the usual. Town's as sleepy as ever."

Sandy gave her a knowing look but didn't push. Instead, she patted the mattress beside her. "Sit with me for a while?"

Mae didn't need to be asked twice. She curled up beside her mother, resting her head gently against Sandy's shoulder. They sat in comfortable silence for a few minutes, just enjoying the stillness, the kind of peace that had grown rare lately.

A few minutes later, John walked in, carrying a small tray with fresh-squeezed lemonade and some shortbread cookies. "I figured we could all use a little something sweet," he said, his voice light as he set the tray on the bedside table.

Sandy chuckled. "You always know how to make an afternoon special."

John sat in the chair beside them, his eyes softening as he took in the sight of his wife and daughter. "We haven't had a lazy afternoon together in a while. Thought we should change that."

Mae looked between them, the moment folding itself into her like a memory she'd never want to forget. She reached for a cookie, breaking it in half and offering a piece to her mother before taking a bite herself.

They talked for hours—about old family vacations, about the time Mae had tried to ride a neighbor's sheep and ended up in the mud, about the high school basketball games where Sandy had cheered the loudest from the stands. The memories wove around them like a warm blanket, wrapping them in a kind of joy that felt untouched by the reality of Sandy's illness.

At one point, Sandy reached for John's hand, threading her fingers through his. "I love you," she murmured, her gaze holding his.

John kissed her knuckles gently. "I love you too, sweetheart."

Mae blinked rapidly, pushing back the sting of emotion. For all the sadness that loomed over them, there was still this—still love, still moments like this to hold onto. And for now, that was enough.

Crystal breezed through the front door just as the last hues of sunset stretched across the sky. Mae, sitting at the kitchen table nursing a cup of tea, barely had time to register her arrival before Crystal's voice filled the quiet space.

"Oh my gosh, Mae," Crystal gushed, setting her purse down on the counter with a dramatic sigh. "I had the *best* afternoon."

Mae glanced up, taking in Crystal's bright-eyed excitement, the unmistakable glow on her face. She was practically vibrating with energy.

"Yeah?" Mae said neutrally, lifting her mug to her lips. "Where'd you go?"

Crystal pulled her hair loose from its ponytail and ran a hand through it, shaking it out as she grabbed a water bottle from the fridge. "Well, I went into town to grab a few things, and guess who I ran into?"

Mae didn't answer. She didn't need to. She already knew. Instead, she kept her gaze steady, waiting.

"Jim," Crystal answered, as if Mae had asked, her smile widening. "And, Mae, we *talked*—really talked. It was like old times, but also... different. Familiar, but *new* in a way, you know?"

Mae set her mug down carefully, forcing her fingers to remain loose around the handle. "That so?"

Crystal sighed dreamily, leaning against the counter as she twisted the cap off her water bottle. "He was so sweet. I mean, not that he wasn't always sweet, but it just felt so easy today. We had lunch on the patio—he made a joke about how he should charge me rent for the amount of time I'm spending at Rocket Ribs." She laughed, taking a sip of her water. "And I told him he could invoice me anytime."

Mae swallowed, the tea suddenly sitting heavy in her stomach. "Sounds nice," she said, keeping her tone even.

"It really was." Crystal sighed, propping her elbow on the counter and resting her chin in her hand. "And you know, I really think there might still be something there. I mean, obviously, we have history, but today, I could *feel* it. The way he looked at me, the way we just fell back into conversation... it's like no time has passed at all."

Mae nodded slowly, her lips pressing together before she spoke. "You think he feels the same way?"

Crystal hesitated, just for a flicker of a moment, but then waved a hand dismissively. "Oh, you know Jim. He's not the type to wear his heart on his sleeve, but I don't know, Mae. I just have a feeling."

Mae hummed in response, taking another slow sip of her tea, willing herself not to react, not to let any of this show. Because it wasn't her place to feel anything. It wasn't her place to care.

Crystal grinned, shaking her head like she couldn't quite believe it herself. "Anyway, I just had to share. It was just... a good day."

Mae exhaled through her nose, offering what she hoped was a convincing smile. "I'm glad."

She wasn't sure if it was a lie.

Crystal stretched with a contented sigh, her energy still bubbling over from her afternoon in town. Then she turned back to Mae with a bright smile. "Oh—by the way, I think we saw you out on your run earlier. Jim and I were sitting outside at the restaurant, and we both tried to call out to you, but you must've had music in your ears. You looked totally in the zone."

Mae's heart gave a small, involuntary stutter, but she kept her expression carefully composed. "Oh. Yeah, I probably didn't hear anything. I had the volume up."

Crystal nodded, unfazed. "You were booking it."

Mae forced a soft laugh, pushing aside the tangle of emotions still lingering beneath the surface.

"How was your day?" Crystal asked, still buoyant.

Mae hesitated only a fraction of a second before responding. "It was good," she said, managing a small but genuine smile. "I got to spend some real quality time with Mom and Dad. Just the three of us. We talked, reminisced, laughed—it felt... important."

Crystal's expression softened, her excitement quieting into something more sincere. "That's really wonderful, Mae. Those moments matter more than anything. You'll be so glad you took the time to be with her."

Mae nodded, her fingers tracing an idle pattern on the countertop. "Yeah, I know. It just—it hit me today how much I need to be present. With everything happening, it's easy to get caught up in worrying about what's next. But today, we were just in the moment. And that meant everything."

Crystal reached over and squeezed Mae's arm lightly. "That's exactly how it should be. No one can predict how much time we have, but we can make the most of what we do. And you're doing that. Just keep showing up for her. That's what she needs most."

Mae swallowed, grateful for the sincerity in Crystal's voice. Whatever past tensions they'd had, whatever misgivings Mae still harbored, in this moment, Crystal was right.

Crystal glanced toward the hallway. "Speaking of which, I should go check on her—make sure she's comfortable and get her settled for the night. I'll check her vitals and go over her evening medications."

Mae nodded, watching as Crystal gathered her supplies with practiced ease. "Thanks, Crystal. For everything."

Crystal smiled over her shoulder as she made her way toward Sandy's room. "Anytime, Mae. That's why I'm here."

As Crystal disappeared down the hall, Mae let out a slow breath, rolling her shoulders to release the tension she hadn't realized she was holding. She was grateful for the day she'd had with her parents. Grateful for the reminder of what mattered most.

That night, the house was still. Even Crystal had gone quiet, her footsteps soft behind the guest room door.

Her phone buzzed with a text from her boss: *Just checking in—any idea when you'll be back online? We're at a tipping point.*

Mae stared at the screen, the words blurring for a moment before she tucked the phone away, unanswered. She had spent years building her career brick by brick, sacrificing weekends, sleep, and sometimes relation-ships. But now, watching her mother drift in and out of shallow sleep, even stepping away for a conference call felt like betrayal. The time she had left wasn't just limited—it was slipping through her fingers.

# Chapter 13

# Jenny's Trip

Mae was jolted awake by the sharp trill of her phone vibrating against the nightstand. Groggily, she reached for it, squinting at the bright screen. Jenny's name flashed across the display. A quick glance at the clock told Mae it was barely past six in the morning. With a groan, she swiped to answer.

"Do you have any idea what time it is?" Mae mumbled, rubbing sleep from her eyes.

"Shoot." Jenny's voice came through, bright and unapologetic. "Time zones. Forgot about those."

Mae sighed, sinking back against the pillows. "It's too early for you to be this awake and chipper. What's up?"

"I have news," Jenny announced, the excitement in her voice unmistakable. "Work is sending me to Austin for a few days."

Mae perked up slightly, running a hand through her tangled hair. "Austin? That's only a couple hours from here."

"Exactly." Jenny paused, as if letting the weight of that sink in. "I'm going to help with a deposition for some billionaire's son and some other heavy hitters. Haven't met him yet, but apparently, he's a big deal. Should be interesting."

Mae hummed, half-listening, still groggy from sleep. "That's... great? I mean, I'm glad you're coming to Texas."

"Well, here's the better part," Jenny continued. "Once I'm done with work, I'm taking a week off. And guess what? I'm coming to see you."

Mae's lips curved into a slow smile. "You are?"

"Of course. What kind of best friend would I be if I didn't come check on you?" Jenny's voice softened, a rare moment of sincerity slipping through. "I know things have been tough. I figured you could use some moral support."

Mae swallowed the lump forming in her throat. "I'd really like that."

Jenny, sensing the shift in Mae's tone, didn't press further. Instead, she cleared her throat and returned to her usual teasing. "Plus, I have to see what kind of trouble you've been getting yourself into. Avoiding Jim like the plague? Watching Crystal prance around him like a lovesick schoolgirl? Sounds like a reality show. I need front-row seats to."

Mae groaned. "Jenny—"

"I'm just saying," Jenny cut in, amusement laced through her words. "I'm going to get to the bottom of this whole 'I don't care about Jim' act you're putting on."

Mae rolled her eyes, shifting to sit up in bed, changing her tone to a whisper to ensure nobody else in the house could hear her. "There's nothing to get to the bottom of. Jim is free to do whatever he wants. And if Crystal thinks there's something between them, that's her business."

Jenny let out an exaggerated sigh. "Right. And I'm the Queen of England."

"Look," Mae said, shaking her head, "this isn't about Jim. My focus is Mom. And Dad. And getting through all of this without completely falling apart."

Jenny's voice softened again. "I know, Mae. And I respect that. But just... promise me you won't shut yourself off from everything else in the process."

Mae hesitated, staring down at the pattern of her quilt. She wanted to argue, to push back, but instead, she exhaled. "I'll try."

Mae traced the edge of her quilt with one finger, wishing she could just shut down the part of her brain that still cared. She didn't want to talk about Jim—not with Jenny, not with anyone. Not when it was easier to pretend he wasn't part of the equation at all.

"Good." Jenny's tone brightened again. "Now, go back to sleep. I'll text you when I land in Austin."

"Please do. And maybe next time, check a clock before you call."

Jenny laughed. "No promises. See you soon, bestie."

Mae hung up, setting her phone back on the nightstand. She sank deeper into the covers, comforted by the thought of Jenny coming.

Meanwhile, the day carried on as usual. By mid-morning, Crystal had already left the house, casually mentioning something about running errands in town. Mae didn't ask. She didn't have to. She already knew exactly where Crystal was going.

**Rocket Ribs. Jim.**

This time, though, Crystal's trip was shorter. When she returned, there was something different about her—her usual bubbly energy dimmed, her smile less effortless. Mae noticed but didn't comment. Instead, she busied herself with folding laundry, pretending not to see the way Crystal lingered near the kitchen, lost in thought.

Mae stayed busy, focusing on helping her father around the house, making sure her mother was comfortable. She reminded herself—again and again—that Jim wasn't her concern.

But that didn't stop the ache in her chest every time she thought of him.

The scent of smoked brisket and warm cornbread filled the house as the doorbell rang, signaling another meal delivery. Mae hesitated for a split second before pulling open the door, revealing Jim standing on the porch, balancing a tray covered in foil-wrapped dishes. He looked as steady and sure as ever, his familiar smile easy but laced with something unreadable.

"Hey, Mae," he said, his voice warm. "Brought dinner. Figured your dad might appreciate another break from cooking."

Mae nodded quickly, stepping aside. "Thanks, Jim. That's thoughtful. Come on in."

She took a step back, already planning her exit, but before she could make her retreat, Crystal emerged from the hallway, her face lighting up when she heard Jim's voice.

"Jim! Twice in one week—you must really be trying to spoil us," she teased, reaching to take the tray from him.

Jim handed it over with a polite chuckle, but his gaze flicked toward Mae, watching as she edged toward the hallway.

"I should check on my mom," Mae murmured, avoiding his eyes.

She didn't wait for a response before slipping away, the sound of Crystal's effortless chatter trailing behind her as she disappeared into Sandy's room. The rhythmic hum of medical equipment greeted her, a familiar comfort against the chaos of her thoughts.

Sandy, propped up against a stack of pillows, studied her daughter with quiet knowing as Mae settled into the chair beside her. "You didn't stay long out there," she observed, her voice gentle.

Mae busied herself by adjusting the blanket over her mother's legs. "Crystal had it covered. Besides, I wanted to check on you. How are you feeling?"

Sandy smiled faintly. "I'm fine, sweetheart. But that's not what I asked."

Mae looked down, smoothing invisible creases in the fabric of the quilt. "I just didn't feel like making small talk."

Sandy gave a knowing hum. "It wasn't about small talk, though, was it?" When Mae didn't answer, she continued, "You and Jim always had something special. Even when you were kids, there was an ease between you two."

Mae let out a short breath, shaking her head. "Mom, it's been years. We're just old classmates now."

Sandy's eyes twinkled with something amused and knowing. "Some people come back into our lives for a reason, Mae."

Mae forced a light laugh, shaking her head. "You sound like a fortune cookie."

Sandy chuckled, then reached for her daughter's hand, giving it a soft squeeze. "I just want you to be honest with yourself. That's all."

Mae bit her lip, dodging the weight of her mother's gaze. "Let's talk about something else. How was your afternoon?"

Sandy allowed the change of subject but the look in her eyes told Mae she wasn't fooled.

Meanwhile, out in the kitchen, John sat at the table as Jim and Crystal continued their conversation. He watched Jim carefully, noting the polite but distant way he responded to Crystal's attempts at playful teasing. Jim wasn't reciprocating much. If anything, John noticed how often his gaze drifted toward the hallway, his easy smile faltering whenever Crystal pulled his attention back.

After a few minutes, Jim cleared his throat. "Well, I should get going. Got an early morning at the restaurant."

Crystal's face fell slightly, but she quickly recovered, flashing him an easy smile. "Of course. Thanks again for dinner."

John leaned back in his chair, his lips pressing into a knowing smile as he watched Crystal attempt to mask her disappointment. He wasn't blind. Jim's interest wasn't where Crystal thought it was. And if his daughter thought she was fooling anyone by pretending not to care—well, she had another thing coming.

Crystal lingered in the kitchen after the door shut, absently stacking the foil trays, her movements slower than usual. She opened the fridge, stared at the shelves like she'd forgotten what she was looking for, then shut it again with a soft sigh.

Something had been off. Jim had smiled, but it hadn't quite reached his eyes. His attention had drifted more than once—to the hallway, to the silence that followed Mae's exit.

Crystal frowned, resting her hand on the counter. For a flicker of a moment, a thought crossed her mind—*Was he looking for Mae? Was that what had pulled him away so easily?*

But no. That didn't track.

Mae hadn't shown even a hint of interest in Jim. If anything, she seemed indifferent, almost cold. Whatever was going on with her, it certainly didn't look like longing. So no, that wasn't it.

He must've had a long day. Probably distracted. Or maybe... maybe he was just trying to play it cool. Hard to get.

Crystal brushed a strand of hair behind her ear, straightening her posture as her expression settled into something more determined.

That was fine. She knew the game. And if Jim wanted to play it, she was more than ready.

Her smile returned—slightly more deliberate this time—as she turned and walked out of the kitchen, her heels clicking with purpose across the tile.

# Chapter 14

# Jenny and the Tycoon's Son

Jenny hadn't expected the oil tycoon's son to be this... normal.

She had spent the last few days in Austin prepping for the deposition, expecting to deal with an entitled, out-of-touch playboy who had more money than sense. The case itself—an investor dispute over land develop-ment—had drawn attention, not just because of the fortune at stake, but because Grant Colton, the heir to the Colton oil empire, had been called in as a key witness.

From the moment he walked into the conference room that morning, he had been poised, articulate, and—to Jenny's surprise—genuinely cooperative. No bravado, no smug indifference, just a man who seemed fully aware of the gravity of the situation and handled it with an easy confidence.

And now, hours later, she found herself sitting across from him at a rooftop bar, the city skyline stretching out behind them, a glass of wine in her hand and a bourbon in his.

"I hope you don't mind me asking you out like this," Grant said smoothly, leaning back in his chair. "But after spending the entire day locked in a boardroom with lawyers, I figured you could use a drink. No business talk, no deposition stress—just good conversation and a strong pour."

Jenny smirked, taking a sip of her wine. "So this was purely for my benefit?"

Grant grinned, tilting his glass toward her. "I'm a gentleman, Jenny. It would've been rude not to invite you."

Despite herself, she laughed. He was good. Smooth, but not in the greasy, well-rehearsed way she had encountered in other high-profile clients. His charm felt effortless, his confidence unforced.

"So, what's next for you after Austin?" Grant asked, watching her over the rim of his glass.

Jenny set her drink down, crossing one leg over the other. "I'm heading to the hill country to see my best friend. She's going through a lot right now, and I figured it's time for a little moral support."

Grant nodded, considering this. "The Texas hill country, huh? It's been a while since I've been out that way."

Jenny raised a brow, already sensing where this was going. "Oh? Thinking about a little getaway?"

Grant smirked. "Maybe. If I had a good reason."

Jenny pretended to think it over, tapping a finger against the stem of her wine glass. "Well, I still have two more days of depositions, but after that I'm heading to Twinsdale. If you're brave enough to follow, you're welcome to come."

Grant raised his glass. "Challenge accepted."

He paused, then added with a grin, "But how about we save your mileage? I'll drive."

Jenny arched a brow. "Oh, you think you're chauffeuring me now?"

"Absolutely," he said smoothly. "It's only fair—I invited myself. Least I can do is get us there in style."

She narrowed her eyes, as if weighing the offer, then smirked. "Only if you let me control the playlist."

"Done," he said, raising his glass again. "But fair warning—I draw the line at boy bands and anything with excessive banjo."

Jenny laughed. "You're going to regret that."

Back in Twinsdale, Mae had lost track of what day it was. The rhythms of hospice care weren't governed by calendars anymore, but by the hiss of the oxygen machine, the muted clink of pill bottles, and the restless pacing from room to room.

Since Jenny's call earlier that week, time had folded in on itself. She wasn't sure if it had been two days or five. All she knew was that Sandy was weaker, Crystal was edgier, and the air in the house was heavy with unsaid things.

That morning, Mae had opened the fridge to find everything rearranged—again. The orange juice was in a different spot, the soup pushed to the back behind a lineup of water bottles, and the leftovers she'd planned to warm for lunch were suddenly missing.

"Guess the fridge has a new system," Mae said lightly, too lightly, as she closed the door with more force than necessary.

From the sink, Crystal didn't look up. "Just trying to keep things from going bad. Some of us notice expiration dates."

Mae let out a small breath through her nose. "Of course."

"Didn't mean anything by it," Crystal added after a beat, still not turning around.

"Didn't say you did," Mae replied, voice even but taut.

The silence that followed wasn't loud, exactly—but it had weight. It stretched across the kitchen like steam from a kettle, hanging in the air until it settled in their shoulders.

She knew she wasn't being fair. Crystal had been doing the bulk of the overnights, and Mae had spent the morning pretending to read emails from her boss without actually opening any of them. There were five flagged messages in her inbox—two marked "urgent." She hadn't responded to any of them. She wasn't ready to admit it, but she could feel the New York pressure creeping in, whispering that she couldn't stay much longer without consequences.

And now, apparently, Jenny was bringing company.

Mae wasn't sure what she had expected when Jenny said she was bringing a guest, but the six-foot-two, broad-shouldered man stepping out of the sleek black SUV was definitely not it.

Grant Colton exuded effortless charm, the kind that came from years of moving through the world with confidence. His designer jeans and polished cowboy boots hinted at wealth, but the way he wore them—casual, unbothered—suggested he didn't have to try. A crisp white button-down stretched perfectly across his broad shoulders, the top two buttons undone just enough to suggest ease rather than arrogance. His slicked-back blonde hair gleamed in the sunlight, styled with just enough effort to look effortlessly cool.

The way he scanned the property with appreciation, his gaze lingering on the sprawling fields and the old wooden fence line, made it clear he wasn't out of his depth. And when he turned to Jenny, flashing her an easy grin, there was no doubt—Grant Colton belonged anywhere he wanted to be, whether that was a boardroom, a country club, or, for the next week, a quiet Texas farmhouse.

"Mae," Jenny called, striding up the driveway. "Meet Grant."

Mae crossed her arms, leveling her best skeptical stare at her best friend. "Grant?"

Grant extended a hand, his grin widening. "Grant Colton. Thanks for letting me crash here for a bit."

Mae shook his hand, her grip firm. "Can't say I had much of a choice, now did I?"

Jenny nudged her playfully. "You'll survive."

John stepped onto the porch, wiping his hands on a rag. His sharp gaze flicked from Grant to Jenny, assessing, measuring, before his expression softened into something welcoming.

Jenny, never one to hesitate, grinned. "And you must be the famous Coach Whitaker," she said, stepping forward before John could extend his hand. Instead of shaking it, she pulled him into a warm hug.

John let out a surprised chuckle but patted her back with a gruff kindness. "Well, now," he said, pulling away and shaking his head. "Didn't see that coming."

Mae laughed. "Dad, this is Jenny. My best friend from New York."

Jenny beamed. "The one and only. And I've heard plenty about you, so I figured a handshake wasn't going to cut it."

John huffed, amused. "Well, any friend of Mae's is welcome here." Then he turned his attention to Grant, his expression settling into something more appraising.

"You two will be staying in the loft above the garage," he said, motioning toward the converted space at the edge of the property. "It hasn't been used in a while, but it's got a couple of beds and a bathroom. Should do just fine."

"Perfect," Grant said easily, tipping his head in gratitude. "I appreciate it, sir."

As Jenny grabbed her bag from the trunk, she shot Mae a soft smile. "I'm really glad I get to be here with you right now."

Mae sighed, already bracing herself. "You say that like I won't put you to work."

Jenny grinned. "I'm counting on it."

The moment Grant stepped into the house, John sized him up the way any protective father would. Grant, to his credit, handled it well, offering a firm handshake and repeating a polite, "Sir, thanks again for letting us crash here for a bit."

John gave a grunt, but there was a glint of something warmer in his eyes—approval, maybe, or at least the start of it. Grant's firm handshake and unassuming manner hadn't gone unnoticed.

"In this house, we treat guests like kin," John said, stepping back. "Make yourself at home."

Grant smiled. "Careful, I've been known to eat my weight in brisket."

John snorted. "Then you'll fit in just fine around here."

John smirked and gestured toward the living room. "Well, come on in, then. I was just about to make a fresh pot of coffee."

As Grant followed John inside, Mae heard her dad ask, "So what do you do when you're not being deposed in boardrooms?"

Grant's easy reply came without hesitation. "Mostly running. If I'm not in a meeting, I'm usually training for my next marathon."

John made an approving noise. "You run? Mae's a runner."

Mae shook her head at the comment but chose not to linger. Instead, she turned toward Jenny, motioning for her to follow. "Come on, let me introduce you to Mom and Crystal."

Jenny sobered slightly, shifting into her more thoughtful, empathetic self. "I'd love that."

Mae led the way down the hall and into her mother's room, where Crystal was adjusting Sandy's blankets, ever meticulous in her care. Sandy's tired eyes lit up when she saw Mae walk in, and even more when she noticed the new face at her side.

"Well, look at you, sweetheart," Sandy murmured. "You brought me company."

Mae smiled and stepped aside, placing a hand on Jenny's shoulder. "Mom, this is my best friend, Jenny Torres. I figured it was about time you two met in person."

Jenny immediately moved to Sandy's bedside, her usual confidence softened by warmth. "It's so nice to finally meet you, Mrs. Whitaker. Mae's told me so much about you."

Sandy's expression turned mischievous. "Oh, I hope it was only the good things."

Jenny laughed. "She worships the ground you walk on, so I'd say you're safe."

Crystal, who had been quietly observing, finally spoke up. "Jenny, it's so nice to meet you. I've heard a lot about you, too."

Jenny turned toward her, her sharp lawyer's gaze pausing briefly on Crystal before offering an easy, practiced smile, "Crystal. Same here."

Crystal returned the smile, but something about the interaction felt... off. Jenny had been polite—gracious, even—but there had been a coolness in her eyes. Not unkind, but measured. As if she were already sizing Crystal up.

Had she said something, done something wrong? She couldn't shake the sense that she'd stepped into some-thing unspoken—like a silent evaluation she hadn't been prepared for.

As Jenny turned her attention back to Sandy, Crystal glanced away, her smile slipping just slightly.

Mae felt the slightest tension between them but decided to ignore it, instead turning back to her mother. "Jenny's going to be staying for the week," she explained. "Dad set up the loft above the garage for her and Grant."

Sandy nodded, her expression thoughtful. "Good. I'm glad you'll have your friend here, Mae. You could use someone to talk to."

Jenny threw Mae a pointed look. "I keep telling her that, but she's stubborn."

Mae sighed. "Alright, alright, let's not gang up on me."

Sandy chuckled, patting Mae's hand. "We're just looking out for you, sweetheart."

Instead, Jenny turned back to Sandy, taking a seat by her bedside. "So, Mrs. Whitaker, tell me—what embar-rasssing stories about Mae do you have stored away? I need new material."

Sandy grinned, settling into her pillow. "Oh, honey, where do I start?"

Mae groaned. "I knew this was a bad idea."

Jenny just smirked. "Too late now."

Mae sighed, but as she looked between her mother and her best friend, she felt a quiet sense of gratitude. Suddenly, she wasn't bracing for the next hit. Whatever else was happening—whatever complicated feelings were stirred in her—right now, this was a moment she could hold onto.

Down the hall, faint laughter echoed from the kitchen—her father's deep chuckle, followed by Grant's lighter reply. The sound drifted toward her, warm and easy, just before the back door creaked shut and muffled it completely.

Mae turned her head toward the sound, a small smile tugging at her lips. If she had to guess, her dad had taken Grant out to the garage to show off the '67 Mustang—his go-to move whenever a male guest passed the initial test. It was practically a rite of passage.

As she glanced toward the kitchen, the smell of her herb bread—rich, warm, and just about done—began to waft through the house, tugging at her attention. Almost tim e for dinner.

# Chapter 15

# Wandering Eyes

"Alright," Jenny said, standing and clapping her hands like a coach calling a timeout. "Time to stop hog-ging your mom, Mae. We've got dinner to serve and a queen to escort to her throne."

Mae raised a brow. "Queen?"

Jenny smirked. "Obviously. Look at her."

Sandy tilted her head, amused. "I thought I was supposed to be the wise elder, not royalty."

"You can be both," Crystal said, entering the room with a folded blanket and a fresh cushion for the wheelchair. "But I agree—it's time you made a cameo at dinner. A little normal never hurt anyone."

Sandy hesitated, her gaze flicking toward the hallway. "I don't want to be a burden."

Jenny rolled her eyes. "You're the main event. No one's eating until you're at the table, so if we all starve, that's on you."

Crystal stifled a laugh as she moved to Sandy's side, her movements gentle and practiced. "Come on. You'll be more comfortable out there. And besides... Mae made her famous herb rolls. You know you can't say no to those."

Sandy looked between the three women—each of them standing there like she was the final vote in a secret council—and let out a sigh that was more fond than frustrated. "Alright, alright. You win. But only if I get a front-row seat to the chaos."

"With popcorn, if we're lucky," Jenny added, already fluffing the throw blanket with dramatic flair.

Together, they eased Sandy into the wheelchair. Crystal took the lead down the hallway, guiding them toward the dining room while Mae dimmed the lights and flipped on the speaker. Soft jazz crackled through the house. The air smelled faintly of garlic and rosemary from the prep Mae had done earlier, but the real cooking was still to come.

The dining room was quiet, almost reverent, bathed in late-afternoon light that filtered in through gauzy curtains. The long table, dusty from disuse, still wore the linen runner Sandy had once loved. Mae gave it a gentle shake while Jenny grabbed a cloth and began wiping down the surfaces with uncommon care.

Sandy chuckled softly as they moved around her. "Are you girls redecorating or making dinner?"

"Both," Crystal said. "This is a full production."

"We're breaking out the good stuff," Mae added, opening the china cabinet with a creak that hadn't been heard in years.

Mae turned, holding up a stack of pristine, gold-rimmed dinner plates like a trophy. "Has this even been used since...?"

"Your graduation party," Sandy said, her voice a little wistful. "I think that was the last time we had it all out."

"Well, it's making a comeback," Mae said, placing it carefully on the sideboard. "Tonight deserves it."

While Crystal started arranging the place settings, Jenny filled water glasses and lit the taper candles in the center of the table. Mae moved toward the kitchen, calling back over her shoulder.

"Alright, Mom—you're in charge now. What's the game plan?"

Sandy raised her eyebrows, amused. "You're deferring to me now?"

"Always have. We just didn't admit it."

With Sandy seated comfortably in the dining room, the women rotated in and out of the kitchen like a tag team—Crystal managing the stovetop, Mae mixing vinaigrette with Sandy directing the proportions from across the room, and Jenny reading recipe instructions aloud with exaggerated flair.

It wasn't just cooking. It was a ritual. Every ingredient passed through laughter, memories, and gentle teasing.

"That's too much salt," Sandy said as Mae lifted the shaker.

"I haven't even started yet," Mae shot back.

"I know. But I've seen your cooking."

"You wound me, ma'am."

It was the kind of easy chaos Mae hadn't felt in years—spoons clattering, napkins being refolded for the third time, Jenny scolding Mae for tasting too much of the dressing. And through it all, Sandy stayed at the center, offering opinions, asking questions, smiling in a way Mae hadn't seen in a long while.

They were just plating the rolls and brushing them with butter when the back door creaked open.

John's voice arrived first, loud and animated. "—and I told him, if you can't tell a flathead from a small-block, you've got no business calling yourself a car guy!"

Grant laughed as they stepped inside, both a little windblown, both wearing that specific kind of grin that men wore after bonding over horsepower and half-finished repairs. There was a streak of grease down John's forearm and a dark smudge on Grant's sleeve—proof of a garage adventure neither had been eager to leave.

Mae looked up from the kitchen with a startled laugh. "You two planning to stay for dinner or start your own auto shop?"

"We almost lost them to the Mustang," Sandy murmured, handing Mae the tongs. "Good timing with dinner."

Crystal gave them both a look. "Wash your hands boys before you start touching anything."

"Yes, ma'am," John said, already moving toward the sink.

"Right behind him," Grant added with a sheepish grin.

Mae caught the look her father gave Grant as he handed him a towel—subtle, approving, solid. The kind of look that didn't need words.

"Dinner smells amazing," Grant said as he dried his hands. "Can I help with anything?"

Sandy, seated at the head of the table, gave him a thoughtful once-over, clearly charmed by the offer. Her smile was warm, but there was a spark of amusement in her eyes. "I like a man who's not afraid to pitch in."

She nodded toward the sideboard. "There's a bottle of red over there that could use uncorking. Think you can handle that?"

Grant grinned. "I've trained for this moment my whole life." He moved toward the sideboard, already scanning for the corkscrew.

John slid into his chair with a satisfied sigh and nodded toward Mae as she set down the final dish. "You didn't tell me the boy knew his way around a carburetor."

Mae raised an eyebrow. "You two were in that garage for over an hour. I figured you were either fixing the Mustang or planning a coup."

"We were fixing the Mustang," John said proudly. "Or at least talking about how to fix it better."

"Which somehow led to a twenty-minute debate about original interiors versus aftermarket upgrades," Grant added, pulling the cork with a quiet *pop*. "For the record, I'm team-original. Nothing beats the soul of factory details."

John gave a satisfied grunt, pointing a fork in his direction. "Finally, someone gets it."

Crystal leaned toward Mae and said under her breath, "Is it weird how excited your dad is right now?"

"Extremely," Mae murmured back, but she couldn't help the smile tugging at her lips.

Grant poured the wine, then handed the bottle to Jenny, who gave him a mock-solemn nod of approval.

"I have to say," she said, "you're surprisingly... normal for the son of a billionaire oil tycoon."

Grant laughed. "That's probably the nicest thing anyone's ever said to me."

Jenny smirked. "Don't get used to it."

The football talk started shortly after everyone dug into the roasted chicken. John brought it up casually—*you ever play?*—and when Grant mentioned he'd been a starting quarterback for a powerhouse team in Austin, everything shifted.

John sat forward in his chair, already elbow-deep in Friday night lights nostalgia. "Wait—Austin Westfield? The Eagles?"

"That's the one."

"Oh, now you've got him going," Sandy said, shaking her head fondly.

"I watched you play once!" John said, pointing a finger like he'd just solved a mystery. "State quarterfinals, back in—what was it—2003?"

Grant blinked, impressed. "You were there?"

"I never forget a good slant route," John said. "You threw one that split three defenders."

Mae leaned toward Crystal. "And now they're best friends."

Crystal smiled. "It's cute, though."

Sandy was quiet for a beat, then looked up with a little smile. "You know," she said, "I still remember when Mae insisted she could throw a tighter spiral than any of the neighborhood boys."

"Oh no," Mae muttered, already sinking into her chair.

"She backed it up, too," Sandy went on. "Launched the ball clear over the fence and straight through the Petersons' kitchen window."

John laughed. "She stood there, mouth open, like she couldn't believe it herself."

Mae groaned. "I thought I was going to be grounded until graduation."

Sandy's eyes sparkled. "Grounded? Your father couldn't stop bragging about it to anyone who'd listen."

Grant glanced across the table at her, eyes full of amusement. "I feel like I missed out on peak Mae."

Mae looked back at him, pretending to glare. "You keep talking like that and you won't get seconds."

"I'm already uncorking wine and talking football with your dad," he said, lifting his glass. "I feel like I'm playing my cards right."

Laughter broke across the table, a kind of lightness Mae hadn't heard in the house in far too long.

She leaned back in her chair, letting the sounds wrap around her—clinking glasses, Sandy's soft laugh, the hum of voices layered over jazz, Grant's easy grin, and her father's rough chuckle rumbling beneath it all. The air felt changed, like the windows had been opened after a long winter.

As laughter swirled around the table—Jenny teasing, Grant holding his own, Crystal chiming in with a rare smile—Sandy shifted slightly in her chair, leaning just a little closer to John beside her.

He didn't speak, just turned his head enough to meet her gaze.

No words passed between them. They didn't need them.

John reached down and gently slid his hand over hers where it rested in her lap.

Sandy's fingers curled around his, soft and slow. Their hands stayed there—still and familiar—as if the gesture had become muscle memory over the decades. But Mae, sitting across from them, felt the shift like a quiet ripple through the room.

Her eyes drifted past them, landing on a framed photo hanging just above their heads on the dining room wall. A black-and-white snapshot from her parents' wedding day—her father in a borrowed suit, her mother radiant in a modest gown, both of them looking at each other like the rest of the world had gone still.

They wore that same look now.

Mae's chest tightened, not painfully, but with a kind of quiet ache she hadn't known she was carrying. That same love—steady, enduring—was still here. Not gone. Not lost. Just quieter now.

Sandy gave John's hand a gentle squeeze, and he returned it without a word.

Then, slowly, Sandy turned her gaze—not away, but toward Mae.

Their eyes met, and for a moment, nothing else moved. No words. No explanations. Just the simple, profound exchange of love between mother and daughter.

Mae held her mother's gaze, committing it to memory—the warmth in her eyes, the soft curve of her smile, the weight of everything they didn't need to say.

*This,* she thought, *is a moment I'll carry with me, always.*

Then Sandy looked back to her plate, and Mae, blinking back the sudden sting in her eyes, let herself breathe it in.

All of it.

As the night wound down, Grant leaned back in his chair, flashing an easy grin. "Can't beat Texas football, that's for sure. Best memories of my life."

John chuckled, nodding in agreement. "Nothing quite like it." He eyed Grant with a newfound respect, then glanced at Mae. "You going for your morning run tomorrow?"

Mae, caught off guard, hesitated before nodding. "Yeah, I was planning to."

Grant perked up. "Mind if I tag along? Could use a change of scenery for my morning workout."

Mae opened her mouth to respond, but Jenny beat her to it. "Oh, she'd love that," she said with a grin, giving Mae a knowing look.

Mae shot her a glare but sighed, resigned. "Sure, if you can keep up."

Grant grinned. "I'll take that challenge."

As they all stood to clear the table, Mae caught Crystal watching Grant thoughtfully, a small, intrigued smile playing on her lips. It didn't go unnoticed.

After Jenny and Grant disappeared up to the loft, John glanced at Sandy as they made their way down the hall to their room. "You know," he said, "that boy's got a good head on his shoulders. Knows his stuff when it comes to classic cars, too. He's not just some spoiled rich kid riding on his family's name — there's something real there."

That night, Mae lay awake longer than she wanted to, staring up at the ceiling as shadows shifted across her room. Her thoughts tangled and pulled in too many directions—her mother's health, her father's sudden lightness, Jenny's watchful gaze, and Grant's easy laughter echoing over dinner. Everything felt softer somehow, but that only made it harder to pin down.

When sleep finally came, it was restless. And by the time the first slivers of dawn crept over the house Mae was already slipping on her running shoes, craving the rhythm and clarity only the road could offer.

# Chapter 16

# A Run and a Glance

She stepped onto the porch, stretching her calves against the wooden railing. The early air was cool and still, the sky tinged with lavender and gold. As she reached down to tie her laces tighter, movement near the garage caught her eye.

Grant stood just outside, already dressed in running gear, rolling his shoulders and adjusting his smartwatch. He hadn't expected her to actually show—but there she was, stretching on the porch, the morning light catching in her hair.

She paused when she saw him, just briefly, like the sight of him unsettled something she hadn't decided how to name. He noticed the way her brow lifted—not unfriendly, just assessing. Guarded, maybe.

He looked up and grinned. "Morning, running buddy."

There was a flicker in his smile, a quiet ask beneath the ease—like he wasn't just running for the Texas scenery. He was still trying to read her. Still wondering what lived behind the long silences and tired smiles.

Mae arched a brow. "How often do you run?"

"Every morning," he replied easily. "You?"

She nodded. "Every morning I can."

Grant's grin widened. Something about the way she said it felt like a small truth offered up. "Well then, let's go."

They started off down the gravel road, their strides naturally syncing. Grant fell into rhythm beside her, letting the silence stretch. She didn't seem like someone who needed to fill space with words. He liked that about her. He liked that she didn't perform her grief. She just carried it—quietly, like a weight she'd grown used to bearing.

Still, he was curious. About the way her eyes kept scanning the horizon. About the tension in her jaw that only loosened when the wind hit her face.

About the way she seemed to be running toward something—or maybe away from it.

He didn't push. Just stayed beside her, calm and steady. Watching. Wondering.

She appreciated this about him—his ability to simply be. But appreciation wasn't affection, and she knew the difference. Whatever ease existed between them came from familiarity, not fire. She glanced sideways at him, noticing the relaxed set of his shoulders, the quiet confidence in his stride.

Once, that might have been enough to stir something. But not now. Not when her thoughts were weighted by too many other things—her mother's fragile health, her father's unspoken heartache, the endless calculations of caretaking. And Jim.

Even when she tried not to think of him, Jim slipped through the cracks. A presence, quiet and persistent, like a shadow across her thoughts—there, then gone, but always returning. The tug was quiet, like a whisper beneath her breath, pulling just enough to remind her he was still there. Somewhere. Waiting, or maybe not. But still *there*.

Grant made a joke about her pace and she laughed, but the sound felt distant to her own ears. She nodded along, engaging just enough to keep the moment from fraying, but her heart wasn't in it.

As they crested the bend in the road, a pickup truck appeared in the distance—Jim's truck. It passed them slow, not quite lingering, but not speeding by either. Mae didn't look directly at the window, but she didn't have to. She felt his eyes. A flicker of something too close to intimacy passed through her, and then he was gone.

Jim spotted them before they noticed him—Mae and Grant, running side by side, their pace easy, movements in sync like they'd done this a hundred times before. She was laughing at something, her head tilted just slightly toward him, and Grant matched her stride with the kind of effortlessness that didn't need words.

The sight hit Jim harder than he expected. A slice of something too close to intimacy. Too comfortable. Too possible. Too right.

His hands tightened on the steering wheel as he passed, keeping his gaze locked on the road ahead. But the image stuck—Mae, smiling in a way he hadn't seen.

A knot twisted in his stomach, slow and sour.

Was this her boyfriend from New York? The one she failed to mention? Was *he* the reason she'd been pulling away?

Jim had told himself it was just timing. She was overwhelmed—taking care of her mom, helping out around the house. Of course she was distant. Of course she was distracted.

But now... maybe it hadn't been about timing at all.

Maybe he'd misread the signals—those glances across the table, the way her knee had brushed his under the booth, the quiet laugh she gave when he paid for her coffee.

Maybe she'd already made her choice. Maybe—he was never actually being considered in the first place.

The kitchen was quiet, still wrapped in the hush of early morning. Sunlight spilled in through the window over the sink, catching on steam rising from freshly poured mugs.

Crystal swirled her coffee, eyes distant for a beat. "He strikes me as the kind of guy who knows exactly what he wants. And doesn't waste time getting there."

Jenny didn't miss the shift in her tone—slightly softer, more personal. She set her mug down and leaned in, just a touch. "He does. And I'm guessing you wouldn't mind being on that list."

Crystal met her gaze without flinching, a small smile playing at her lips. "Can you blame me?"

Jenny chuckled. "Not even a little."

There was a beat of silence, easy but charged.

"If you're curious," Jenny added, cocking her head, "why not ask him yourself?"

Crystal lifted her cup, taking another sip like she had all the time in the world. "Maybe I will."

Jenny grinned behind her mug, hiding the spark of amusement in her eyes. *This is going to be fun,* she thought.

Outside, the quiet of the morning was broken by the crunch of gravel under running shoes. Mae and Grant rounded the corner of the street, their breaths still a little uneven, cheeks flushed from the run and the early morning chill. As they slowed to a walk, the quiet hum of the countryside settling around them like a soft quilt.

Jenny was already leaning in the doorway, mug in hand, one brow arched and a knowing smile tugging at her lips.

"Well, look who decided to be productive before sunrise," she called out.

Mae rolled her eyes as she stepped onto the porch. "It wasn't that early."

Grant grinned. "Just early enough to feel smug about it."

Jenny snorted. "Don't hurt yourselves patting your own backs."

Grant laughed, then tipped his head toward the driveway. "I'm gonna grab a shower in the loft before breakfast. See you in a bit?"

He gave Mae a quick nod and jogged off toward the garage, the crunch of gravel trailing behind him.

The second it shut behind him, Jenny grabbed Mae by the arm, and pulled her toward the front porch without a word.

Mae barely had time to protest before they landed side by side on the porch swing, Jenny already grinning like she knew *exactly* what she was doing.

"Okay," she said, handing Mae a mug of coffee, all cream and sugared up, just the way she liked it. "Spill."

Mae took it, eyeing her warily. "Spill what?"

Jenny tilted her head, all mock innocence. "Oh, I don't know... maybe how you and Mr. Marathon looked like you were one slow jog away from holding hands out there?"

Mae rolled her eyes. "There's nothing to spill. We ran. We talked. That's it."

Jenny raised an eyebrow but said nothing.

Mae took a sip of her coffee, then added, "Look... he's charming. He's interesting. But there wasn't a spark. Not like *that*."

Jenny studied her for a beat, then nodded slowly. "Good."

Mae blinked. "Good?"

Jenny smirked. "Yes. Because—Crystal."

Mae frowned. "What about Crystal?"

Jenny leaned in, lowering her voice like they were sharing state secrets. "Crystal has a little something going on for Grant. I saw it yesterday. The look, the body language, the whole thing."

Mae stared at her. "You're serious?"

Jenny sat back, clearly enjoying herself. "Dead serious. And I think we, as loyal and supportive women of taste, should help that story along."

Mae nearly choked on her next sip. "Excuse me?"

"Oh, come on," Jenny said, waving a hand. "You've seen the way she looks at him. And let's be honest, Grant's got that whole 'Texan charmer with money' thing going for him. They're practically made for each other."

Mae wasn't sure whether to be amused or skeptical. Crystal had spent the past two weeks trying to rekindle something with Jim, yet now she was shifting gears? "I don't know," Mae hedged. "Crystal seems pretty set on Jim."

Jenny scoffed. "Please. If she was really making progress with Jim, do you think she'd be eyeing Grant like he's the last piece of pecan pie at Thanksgiving? No, she's realizing Jim isn't biting, and she's looking for an alternative."

Mae sighed, rubbing her temple. "Even if you're right, what exactly do you propose? A forced date? A candlelit dinner and a conveniently stranded car so they have to spend the evening together?"

Jenny's grin widened. "Now you're thinking like me," she said mischievously.

Mae shook her head but couldn't help the amused smile that tugged at her lips. "I still don't get why you're not the one interested in Grant. The guy's single, rich, good-looking. You two spent hours in a car together—don't tell me there wasn't at least a flicker of interest."

Jenny laughed, leaning back against the swing. "Oh, there was a flicker, all right. I had big plans for this weekend, trust me. Until we had a little heart-to-heart somewhere around mile marker fifty. Turns out, Grant's looking to settle down, find someone who wants to plant roots in Texas."

Mae raised an eyebrow. "And you don't?"

Jenny scoffed. "Mae, my heart is in New York. My family, my career, everything I've worked for—it's all there. The energy of the city, the late-night takeout, the rush of working in high-profile litigation? That's what I love. Austin's nice, but it's not home."

She paused, then added, more quietly, "And honestly? I respect the hell out of Grant. He knows who he is. What he wants. The last thing I'm gonna do is waste his time with something that has an expiration date stamped all over it."

Mae nodded slowly.

Jenny took another sip of her coffee, stretching her legs out in front of her. "Besides, he and Crystal actually make sense. She's been looking for stability, and Grant is stability wrapped in a perfectly tailored and starched button-down. So why not give fate a little nudge?"

Mae studied her friend for a long moment, then sighed. "I have a feeling this is going to be entertaining at the very least."

Jenny grinned, raising her coffee cup in a mock toast. "That's the spirit."

Before Mae could respond, her phone buzzed on the porch railing. A glance at the screen made her stomach twist—New York number. Her boss.

She hesitated, then picked up. "Hey, Marc."

"Mae! Hope I'm not catching you at a bad time," Marc said, his tone pleasant but firm. "Just checking in since your two weeks are up. We need to start planning for your return."

Mae sat up straighter, gripping her coffee cup a little too tightly. Two weeks. Had it really been that long? "Right. Of course."

"Look, I know things have been tough, and we all understand family stuff," Marc continued. "But we're closing in on a big deadline. I need to know what your plan is."

A plan. That was the problem. She didn't have one.

"I'll... let you know soon," Mae said finally.

Marc paused, then sighed. "Alright, but don't wait too long. We need you back, Mae."

The call ended, leaving Mae staring at her phone, her fingers wrapped tightly around it as if holding onto something slipping away. She hadn't thought about work in days, hadn't checked her emails, hadn't even considered booking a flight back. The thought of returning to that life—a life that suddenly felt worlds away—left a strange, hollow feeling in her chest.

Jenny, who had been watching quietly, finally spoke. "You okay?"

Mae exhaled sharply, setting her phone down on the porch floorboards. "He didn't even ask."

"Ask what?"

"How my mom's doing. How I'm doing. Anything, really." She let out a humorless laugh. "Just deadlines, projects, and making sure I get back in time to keep everything running smoothly. Like I'm a damn cog in a machine."

Jenny tilted her head, studying Mae carefully. "And how does that make you feel?"

Mae scoffed. "Like maybe if they don't care about me, I shouldn't care about them either. Why should I be concerned about their deadlines and needs when they clearly don't give a second thought about mine?" She shook her head, gripping her coffee cup tighter. "I've spent years putting my job first. Staying late, picking up extra work, never saying no. And now, when I finally take time off for something that actually matters, I realize... I'm completely replaceable to them."

Jenny sighed, leaning back against the porch swing. "Maybe it's not about being replaceable. Maybe it's about realizing that your life doesn't have to revolve around a job that wouldn't blink if you left."

Mae stared out at the horizon, the morning sun casting long shadows across the yard. "I thought my life was in New York. But now... I don't know. Maybe it never really was."

Jenny didn't say anything, just sipped her coffee and let Mae sit with the weight of her own words. Because sometimes, the hardest truths were the ones you had to realize on your own.

Inside, Grant's easy laughter carried from the kitchen, and Crystal's voice followed, light and engaging. Mae glanced toward the door, watching as Grant leaned against the counter, talking animatedly about something while Crystal listened, her expression rapt.

Jenny nudged Mae with her elbow. "See? That right there. Tell me they don't look good together."

Mae forced a small smile, unwilling to admit that Crystal's attention was somewhere other than Jim. Maybe Jenny's little scheme wasn't so far-fetched after all.

# Chapter 17

# A Little Nudge from Sandy

Mae and Jenny stepped inside from the porch, the lingering warmth of the morning sun fading as they moved through the hallway toward Sandy's room. The scent of lavender and the soft hum of medical equipment filled the space, wrapping them in an air of quiet comfort.

Sandy looked up from where she rested, her eyes brightening at the sight of Jenny. "Well, if it isn't my other daughter," she teased, reaching out a hand.

Jenny grinned, taking Sandy's frail but warm hand in both of hers. "You know, if you keep calling me that, I might just have to start making holiday plans down here."

"Wouldn't be the worst thing in the world," Sandy said with a wink, then turned her gaze to Mae. "You two were out on the porch an awfully long time. Should I be worried?"

Mae smirked. "Jenny's up to something, as usual."

Sandy chuckled. "That doesn't surprise me one bit."

Jenny feigned innocence. "I am simply trying to help certain people see what's right in front of them."

Before Mae could protest, the door creaked open, and Crystal stepped inside, clipboard in hand. "Morning, Sandy. Just checking on your vitals. How are we feeling today?"

Sandy smiled. "Oh, about the same. But I was just having a lovely chat with the girls about how nice it is to have company around here. It's not often we get such a lively bunch."

Crystal checked the IV line, nodding as she noted something on her clipboard. "It's been nice having a full house, I imagine."

Sandy glanced at Jenny before giving Crystal a knowing look. "Especially with Grant around. He seems like a fine young man. You two have a lot in common, don't you? Austin, UT, big city living?"

Crystal paused, her professional demeanor flickering just slightly. "I suppose we do. He sure is easy to talk to."

"Well, that's important," Sandy said lightly. "And not bad to look at either, she said with a wink."

"Mother," Mae gasped.

"I'm just saying." Sandy said with a smile, noticing Crystal blushing.

Mae watched the exchange, hiding her amusement behind her coffee cup. She didn't know whether to laugh or frown. Her mother had always been good at seeing people clearly—sometimes too clearly.

Jenny, however, shot Mae a victorious look. She wasn't meddling. She was just speeding up the inevitable.

Crystal gave a small, awkward smile. "I'll... keep that in mind." She turned back to her chart a little too quickly, but the smile lingered, softer now, like the idea had taken root.

As Crystal finished up, Sandy turned her attention back to Mae. "Sweetheart, will you stay for a bit? I'd like to talk with you."

Jenny took the hint, squeezing Mae's shoulder before standing. "I'll go find Grant and see if he needs a tour of the town. Crystal, want to tag along?"

Crystal hesitated but nodded. "Sure."

As the door closed behind them, Sandy exhaled, studying Mae for a moment. "You're still running, aren't you?"

Mae frowned. "Running? Well, ya, I just got back from my morning jog."

"I'm not talking about those morning jogs," Sandy said, her voice gentle but firm. "You're running from your feelings."

Mae sighed, crossing her arms. "Mom—"

"No, let me say this," Sandy interrupted. "I see the way you react when his name comes up. And I saw the way you made yourself disappear when he came by with dinner the other night."

Mae looked down, tracing a finger over the edge of the nightstand. "Mom, Jim is free to be with whoever he wants. I have no claim on him, and the last thing I want is to start a civil war in this house, over some guy."

Sandy reached out, her hand resting over Mae's. "Maybe not. But that doesn't mean you don't want to."

Mae bit her lip, emotions swirling inside. "It's just so complicated."

Sandy squeezed her hand. "Life always is. But the real question is—what do you want?"

Mae opened her mouth to answer but hesitated as she tilted her head and dawned a confused look on her face. What did she want?

Sandy's knowing smile returned. "Just think about it, sweetheart. That's all I ask."

Mae exhaled and nodded. "Okay. I will."

As they sat in a quiet moment of companionship, Sandy patted Mae's hand. Across the room, Jenny's voice rang from the front door, her laughter mixing with Grant's deep chuckle.

Mae glanced toward the window, watching as Crystal stepped outside with them, her posture lighter than before. Mae turned back to her mother, whose lips curved into the smallest, most knowing smile.

Mae paused, her eyes resting on the gentle rise and fall of her mother's chest. Morning light filtered through the curtains, casting a soft glow across Sandy's face—illuminating the quiet resilience that had held their family together for years. She opened her mouth, then closed it again, unsure. The call from her boss earlier that morning still echoed in her mind, full of implications she wasn't ready to face alone. What she wanted—what she needed—was her mother's advice. Her steady voice. Her clarity.

"Mom, I got a call from Marc this morning" Mae finally said, her voice quiet. "My boss in New York."

Sandy opened her eyes, studying Mae with a gentle but knowing gaze. "And what did he have to say?"

"He reminded me that my two weeks are up," Mae admitted, twisting her hands together. "He expects me to go back soon."

Sandy didn't react immediately, instead taking a slow, steady breath. "And what do you want to do?"

Mae exhaled sharply. "I don't know. I haven't thought about work since I got here. And honestly? I don't think work has thought much about me either." She paused, shaking her head. "Marc didn't even ask about you. Or Dad. Or how I was doing. It was all about deadlines and expectations. And for the first time, I just... I don't feel guilty for not caring."

Sandy gave a small, tired smile. "Maybe that tells you something, sweetheart."

Mae looked down, letting the words settle. Maybe it did.

After a moment, Sandy reached for the worn Bible resting on the nightstand. "Why don't you read to me for a bit?"

Mae nodded, taking the book from her mother's hands. Before she opened it, Sandy closed her eyes and whispered a small prayer. "Lord, guide my daughter as she stands at a crossroads. Help her find clarity, strength, and peace in the path You have set before her."

The words settled into Mae's heart, soothing in their simplicity. She exhaled and let her fingers brush over the delicate pages before letting them fall open at random. Her eyes skimmed over the passage in front of her, and she began to read aloud.

**"'Trust in the Lord with all your heart, and do not lean on your own understanding. In all your ways acknowledge Him, and He will make straight your paths.'"**

The room was silent for a moment, save for the steady hum of the medical equipment playing like a hymn in the background. Sandy smiled, a deep contentment settling over her face. "Sounds like an answer to me."

Mae let out a soft chuckle, shaking her head. "Or a reminder."

Sandy squeezed Mae's hand. "Sometimes, reminders are exactly what we need."

Mae sat there, letting the words soak in, knowing deep down that this was a conversation she wasn't finished having—not with her mother, and not with herself.

As Mae closed the Bible, the weight of the passage she had just read settled over her like a quiet revelation. She didn't have answers yet, but the words left behind a sense of reassurance. She looked up to find her mother watching her intently, a soft, knowing expression in her eyes.

Before either of them could speak, the door creaked open, and John stepped in, a cup of coffee in his hand. He took in the peaceful scene—his wife tucked under her blankets, their daughter sitting beside her, the worn Bible resting in Mae's lap—and smiled gently.

"Morning, ladies," he greeted, his deep voice carrying the warmth of familiarity. "Everything alright in here?"

Mae met his gaze and hesitated before nodding. "Yeah. We were just talking... about some decisions I need to make."

John set his coffee down on the bedside table and took a seat in the chair by Sandy's side. He looked between them, concern flickering across his face. "Decisions, huh? This about work? Or... something else?"

Sandy reached for John's hand, giving it a light squeeze. "Mae's boss called. Her leave is up, and he wants her back in New York."

John's expression darkened slightly, but he kept his voice even. "I see. And what do you want to do, sweetheart?"

Mae exhaled, rubbing her fingers over the cover of the Bible. "I... don't know. New York has been my life for so long. My job, my apartment, my routine. But being here... it's different. I haven't even thought about work until he called, and when he did, he didn't even ask how I was doing. It was just deadlines and expectations."

John nodded slowly. "That tells you something, doesn't it?"

Mae chewed her lip, not ready to say it out loud. Instead, she tilted her head, studying her father. "Dad, you've been watching everything happening in this house. What do you think?"

John leaned back slightly, considering his words. "I think you've got a lot to figure out. But I also think there's something—or someone—you might not be admitting to yourself."

Mae frowned. "What do you mean?"

John glanced at Sandy, who gave him a small, knowing nod. He turned back to Mae. "Jim Carter?"

Mae stiffened, "Not you too."

But John pressed on gently. "I saw him looking for you the other night. When you left the room after answering the door, his eyes followed you. And let me tell you something else—I've watched that boy long enough to know when a man isn't interested in a woman. And Jim? He's not interested in Crystal."

Mae opened her mouth, but nothing came out. She felt Sandy's gentle gaze on her as the weight of her father's words settled in.

"Mae," John continued, his voice kind but firm, "sometimes, the best things in life don't come in the package you expected. And sometimes, you have to slow down long enough to see what's been right in front of you all along."

Mae swallowed hard, her heart pounding. Was she really ready to admit the truth she had been pushing away for weeks? And if she did, what would she do about it?

# Chapter 18

# Dinner Out

The sun was dipping low over Twinsdale when Jenny, Grant, and Crystal pulled back into the driveway, the scent of fresh air and fresh cut grass clinging to them. Mae had spent the afternoon in quiet conversation with her parents, but as soon as she heard the car doors slam, she braced herself.

Jenny was the first to bound up the patio steps, her eyes bright with excitement as she entered the screen door and half ajar front door. "Mae?"

"In here," Mae replied from her parent's room.

"Alright, I have to say—cute town. Very small. But cute," Jenny announced, tossing her bag full of shopping conquests onto the floor in the foyer. "And I have one very important question... where's the best place to eat?" As she walked into Sandy's room, finding Sandy, John and Mae.

Mae smirked. "You mean you spent the entire afternoon in town and didn't find a place to eat?"

Jenny gasped in mock offense. "I was soaking up the local charm! You should see all the cute things I found. But now, I'm starving." She turned to Grant and Crystal who had just caught up with her, entering the small bedroom. "Tell her."

Grant chuckled, slipping his hands into his pockets. "She's not wrong. I could eat. I noticed a barbecue joint in town—Rocket Ribs, I think? I always like to try local barbecue spots."

Crystal perked up instantly, her lips curling into an eager smile. "That's Jim's place! We should definitely go. Best barbecue in town." She turned to Mae and her parents expectantly. "Right?"

It wasn't just the brisket or the buzz about the food—it was the chance. However small. Maybe tonight he'd see her in a different light.

Mae caught the look in Crystal's eyes and hesitated, but she could already see Jenny's wheels turning. "I—"

"Perfect!" Jenny cut in, clapping her hands together. "That settles it. We're going."

John chuckled, catching Mae's hesitation. "It's just dinner, sweetheart. No harm in getting out for a bit. I'll hold down the fort here."

Mae exhaled, glancing at her mom. Sandy gave her a reassuring smile, her voice gentle. "Go on, honey. Enjoy yourself."

With no way out, Mae reluctantly agreed. "Fine. But if Jenny starts scheming, I'm walking home."

With that, Jenny locked arms with Mae and started pulling her out the door. "Want us to get you guys something Mr. and Mrs. Whitaker?" she said as she turned back in deference.

"No, we still have leftovers from the other night. We'll be just fine." John said, walking the group to the front door.

By the time they arrived at Rocket Ribs & BBQ, the dinner rush was winding down. Jim was at the counter, sleeves rolled up, speaking with one of his staff members as they wiped down and straightened up the glasses and bottles behind the bar. The moment Mae stepped inside, his gaze lifted—lingering on her just long enough for her stomach to tighten and her body to jolt with a flash of heat.

Crystal, oblivious, breezed past her and straight toward the counter. "Hey, stranger. Hope you saved us a good table."

Jim offered a polite smile, but his eyes flickered back toward Mae before he responded. "What a surprise! Got the perfect one for you guys over here," he said, pointing to a table on the patio next to the open bonfire pit.

Jenny and Grant followed Crystal to their seats, but Mae held back. Jim took the opportunity to step closer, his voice low.

"Didn't think I'd see *you* here tonight."

Mae offered a small smile, determined to keep things light. "Neither did I."

Jim hesitated, then added, "Saw you out running this morning—with that guy. Is this... your boyfriend?"

Mae blinked, caught off guard. "Grant? Oh—no. Definitely not."

Before he could ask anything more, Jenny piped up from the table. "Oh Jim, so are ribs the best thing on the menu?"

Jim smirked, tearing his gaze from Mae. "Yeah, I'm definitely biased toward them. But the brisket's pretty amazing too."

He disappeared into the kitchen, the screen door creaking softly behind him. A moment later, he returned with a tray of steaming cups, the rich aroma of freshly brewed coffee rising in warm spirals.

The scent mingled with the smoky sweetness of brisket and the earthy burn of post oak wood smoldering in the fire pit. The bonfire crackled steadily from a wide, circular stone pit built into the center of the patio, casting golden light across the gathering. Embers glowed beneath the logs, sending the occasional spark drifting upward into the night air.

Jim moved between the tables, setting cups down with quiet ease. When he reached Mae, he paused just slightly.

"This one's for you," he said, setting the mug gently in front of her.

Mae raised an eyebrow. "For me?"

Jim nodded, his voice warm with amusement. "Told you I'd take your challenge seriously. Cherry wood-smoked coffee. Smooth, creamy without cream, and something I think you'll appreciate—if you drink it black first."

The group watched as Mae hesitated, then lifted the cup to her lips. She blew on it, hesitated, then brought it back to her lips and blew gently—slowly again, almost reluctantly. She never drank black coffee. Too bitter. Too harsh.

The moment the coffee hit her tongue, warmth bloomed through her, the smoky richness balanced by a subtle sweetness. She blinked in surprise, then took another sip. "Wow."

Jim's grin widened. "That a good wow?"

Mae nodded. "More than good. You actually did it. It's smooth—like really smooth. I could actually drink this black."

Jenny let out an exaggerated gasp. "Wait, hold on. Mae Whitaker is drinking black coffee? Jim, you may have just altered the course of history."

Laughter filled the table as the group sampled the coffee and Crystal subtly watching the way Jim and Mae interacted. Mae, too caught up in the moment, didn't notice Crystal's gaze, but Jenny picked up on it.

"Let's order shall we?" Jenny piped in.

Jim exclaimed, "I've got you covered."

Jim proceeded to bring out platter after platter of wonderful barbecue. First course, an appetizer platter of smoked chicken wings and burnt ends. Then came the main course – a full rack of baby back ribs, two pounds of brisket, smoked turkey breast and three flavors of hot links. The meat was joined with sides of smoked mac and cheese, grilled brussel sprouts, coleslaw and pit beans.

Grant couldn't stop raving about the fare served. "This ranks up there with the best barbecue in Austin, that's for sure. Maybe some of the best in Texas."

As dinner was wrapping up, a light drizzle began to fall, tapping gently against the tin roof of the restaurant. The group, laughing and relaxed from their meal, retreated inside to the back room, stopping at the bar to grab a few frosty Shiner Bock beers and some cold margaritas on the rocks. The room was warm and inviting, a string of dim lights casting a golden glow over the pool table at its center. The scent of cedar mixed with post oak smoke lingered in the air.

The room was warm and inviting, a string of dim Edison bulbs casting a soft, golden glow over the space. Center stage was a striking pool table, its base crafted from thick, weathered logs and trimmed with carved Lone Star emblems on each side. The black felt surface stood in rich contrast to the golden wood, giving the whole piece a rugged elegance that fit the space perfectly.

Behind it, a large Texas flag hung proudly on the corrugated metal wall, its bold red, white, and blue adding a punch of color to the otherwise earthy palette. The scent of cedar mingled with post oak smoke, curling through the room like a familiar memory.

A dartboard was mounted, surrounded by weathered barnwood on one of the walls, and in the corner, a retro Miss Pac-Man arcade machine blinked beside a worn leather stool. A shuffleboard table ran along the far side of the room, and a pair of repurposed whiskey barrels served as side tables, their lacquered tops gleaming beneath the warm light.

It was the kind of room that didn't take itself too seriously—full of comfort, competition, and a whole lot of Texas soul.

Grant and Jenny were already at the pool table, racking up the balls for the first round, their easy banter filling the space. Jenny lined up a shot, playfully nudging Grant with her hip as he teased her about her last missed attempt. Mae lingered near the edge of the room, nursing the initial sips of her margarita.

Crystal, however, stood quietly beside her, shifting her weight from one foot to the other. Mae caught the movement from the corner of her eye just as Crystal leaned in, lowering her voice.

"Mae... I need to tell you something."

Mae straightened, sensing the change in Crystal's tone. "What is it?"

Crystal exhaled, running a hand through her hair. "Jim. He's been... distant with me. No matter how hard I try, he just won't engage. And tonight—" she hesitated, glancing across the room to where Jim stood near the bar talking to some of his customers. "I see it now. He's not interested in me. But he is definitely interested in you."

Mae felt her pulse quicken, and her face flush. "Crystal—"

Crystal shook her head before Mae could say anything more. "Don't deny it. I know what I saw. The way he looks at you? It's different. And honestly? I think I'm okay with it."

Mae blinked, caught off guard. "You are?"

Crystal let out a quiet laugh, her lips quirking into a small, wry smile. "Yeah. I think I am. I mean, don't get me wrong—I wanted it to work with Jim. I really did. But it was always me trying, and him... well, not. And Grant—" she paused, her eyes flickering to the other side of the room where Grant was gesturing animatedly as he recounted some story that had Jenny rolling her eyes. "Grant's different. He's got this presence about him, and for the first since I arrived back in Twinsdale, I feel like I'm not chasing something that isn't there."

Mae followed her gaze, watching as Grant turned to say something to Crystal, his easy grin reaching all the way to his eyes. There was no doubt that he was charming, but there was also something steady about him—something that seemed to have caught Crystal's full attention.

Mae struggled to find the right words, her thoughts tangled. But before she could say anything, Crystal gave her a knowing look, stepping back toward the pool table with a smirk. "Looks like it's your break, Mae."

Mae swallowed hard, gripping the edge of the pool table for something solid to hold onto. As she picked up the cue stick, beginning to chalk the tip, she felt the weight of the moment settle over her. Maybe Crystal was right. Maybe Jim had never been waiting for Crystal at all.

Maybe, all along, it had been Mae.

CRACK! Three balls fell into pockets. Mae strutted around the table, smirking with a newfound confidence. "Looks like we're solids, Jenny."

As the night wore on, Jim kept popping in to check on drinks and to chit-chat with the group. Grant and Jim hit it off immediately, swapping stories about barbecue joints from Twinsdale to Austin and from Dallas to Houston.

Through it all, Jim kept stealing glances at Mae, sensing a shift in her demeanor. Something was different—lighter, freer. The smile she gave him wasn't forced, wasn't guarded. It was just... Mae. And though he kept his distance, not pressing, not pushing, he felt something settle.

Hope.

That night, back at the house, Mae sat at her mother's bedside, recounting the evening's events. The soft glow of the bedside lamp cast a warm halo around them, flickering gently as if in tune with the rhythmic hum of the medical equipment. Sandy listened with a gentle smile, her fingers lightly tapping against Mae's hand as she absorbed every detail.

"So, Crystal finally admitted it," Mae murmured, absently smoothing a wrinkle in the blanket. "She sees now that Jim isn't interested in her. And apparently, she's decided Grant is worth pursuing instead."

Sandy chuckled softly. "That girl's always been quick on her feet. But I'd say she's right about one thing—Jim's eyes have never strayed far from you."

Mae swallowed, shaking her head as she leaned back in the chair. "I don't know, Mom. Maybe he was just being polite. Maybe I'm reading too much into things."

Sandy gave her daughter a knowing look. "Mae, when are you going to stop talking yourself out of your own happiness?"

Mae's gaze dropped to her lap, her fingers toying with the edge of the blanket. "It's not that simple."

"Of course, it isn't," Sandy said, her voice calm but unwavering. "Nothing worth having ever is. But tell me this—when you think about going back to New York, back to your job, your apartment, does it feel right? Or does it feel like leaving something unfinished?"

Mae hesitated, caught off guard by how quickly her throat tightened. She thought about Marc's phone call earlier that morning, the impatience in his voice, the complete lack of concern for anything beyond her productivity. She thought about the skyline she once adored, the busy streets, the late nights in the office that had once felt fulfilling. But now? The thought of slipping back into that routine felt... empty.

"I don't know what I'm doing," Mae admitted, her voice barely above a whisper. "I don't know where I belong anymore."

Sandy reached for her hand, squeezing it softly. "Sweetheart, happiness isn't about always knowing the answer. It's about being brave enough to find out."

Mae exhaled, the weight of uncertainty pressing down on her. But as she sat there, bathed in the quiet comfort of her mother's presence, she felt something shift—like a door cracking open, letting in a sliver of light.

Sandy's eyes softened. "You have time, Mae. You don't have to decide everything tonight. Just promise me you'll listen to your heart."

Mae nodded, her throat tight. "I promise."

Her mother smiled, brushing a strand of hair from Mae's face. "That's my girl. Now, go get some rest. Tomorrow will bring its own answers."

Mae lingered a moment longer, pressing a kiss to Sandy's forehead before slipping out of the room. As she stepped into the dimly lit hallway, she let out a slow breath. She wasn't sure where she was going—but maybe, just maybe, she was finally ready to stop running.

# Chapter 19

# The Quiet After

Fog set in thick the morning Sandy passed away. It rolled in before dawn, swallowing the landscape in a dense, muted gray. The lawns that stretched beyond the house disappeared beneath its heavy cloak, as if the world itself had paused, holding its breath.

Mae woke to the stillness, an eerie kind of quiet that settled deep in her bones before she even opened her eyes. The night had been long, restless, and filled with the weight of a truth she wasn't ready to face. And yet, deep down, she knew. Knew before she reached the door, before she made her way down the hall to her mother's room, before she saw the way her father sat beside the bed, his head bowed, his hands wrapped gently around Sandy's.

The air was thick, weighted with love and loss. The hum of machines that had been a steady background noise for weeks had gone silent. Now, the only sound was the steady ticking of the clock on the nightstand, marking time that had already run out.

John lifted his gaze when Mae stepped inside, his eyes red-rimmed but steady. "She's gone, sweetheart."

The words didn't hit all at once. They drifted in like the fog outside, slow and inevitable, settling into the empty spaces of her heart. Mae felt her knees threaten to give, but she willed herself forward, sinking into the chair beside her father. She reached for Sandy's hand, curling her fingers around the warmth that had yet to fade. Her mother's face was soft, peaceful—serene in a way Mae hadn't seen in a long time. As if she had simply drifted into a dream she would never wake from.

A lump rose in Mae's throat, thick and heavy. She had known this moment was coming. She had braced for it. But knowing didn't make it easier. Nothing could. Because how do you say goodbye to the woman who shaped you, who loved you before you even knew what love was? How do you let go of the person who had been your constant, your home, your heart?

Tears welled, slipping down her cheeks, but she didn't wipe them away. Instead, she leaned in, pressing a trembling kiss to her mother's forehead. "I love you, Mama," she whispered, the words catching in her throat. "Always."

John let out a shuddering breath, his grip on Sandy's hand tightening before he exhaled slowly, releasing it. "She was ready," he murmured. "She told me last night. Said she wasn't scared. Said she felt at peace."

Peace. The word lingered in the air, wrapping around Mae like a gentle embrace. It was what Sandy deserved, what she had always given to the people she loved—a soft place to land, even in the hardest of times.

Crystal appeared in the doorway, her eyes glassy, her voice quiet. "I'll take care of everything. I'll start making phone calls. Give you guys some time."

John nodded, but his focus remained on Sandy, his fingers ghosting over her knuckles one last time. "We should take a moment," he said. "Before anything else, just... a moment."

So they did. In the hush of the morning, as the fog swirled outside and the sun fought to break through, they sat together, bound by love and loss, wrapped in the kind of silence that only comes when a heart has been forever changed.

Mae's mind drifted as she held her mother's hand, remembering the last conversation they had. It had been late, the room dimly lit by the soft glow of the bedside lamp. Sandy had smiled, her eyes filled with a quiet knowing. "You're stronger than you think, Mae. You always have been."

Mae had shaken her head, blinking away tears. "I don't feel strong."

Sandy's hand had squeezed hers, gentle but firm. "You will. One day, you'll look back and realize you carried more than you ever thought you could. And when that day comes, I want you to remember something."

Mae had waited, her throat tight. "What?"

Sandy had smiled again, weaker this time. "That I will always be with you. In the way you laugh, in the way you love, in the way you fight for the people who matter. I will always be here."

Now, as Mae sat beside her mother's still form, those words echoed inside her, a quiet promise that would live on even in the emptiness. She closed her eyes, trying to capture the moment, to sear it into memory before time could take it away.

Mae didn't know how long they sat there—minutes, maybe more. The world outside the fog had kept turning, even as hers stood still.

Beside her, John shifted in his chair, the worn cushion creaking under his weight. He straightened slowly, then leaned back in his chair with a tired breath and quiet tears streaming down his face. For a moment, he just stared at Sandy, his expression unreadable.

Then, quietly, he reached over and slid his hand into Mae's, his grip steady despite the tremble in his fingers.

"She was so proud of you, you know."

Mae swallowed hard, nodding. "I hope so."

Crystal appeared in the doorway a few minutes later, her voice soft in a hushed tone, and her voice cracking. "They'll be here soon. But there's no rush."

Mae nodded, wiping at her cheeks. "I just... I don't know how to walk out of this room without her."

The weight of it hit her as soon as she said it. Walking out meant leaving her mother behind. Not just the still, quiet figure in the bed—but the voice that soothed her nightmares, the laugh that filled a kitchen, the steady hand on her back when the world spun too fast.

How was she supposed to cross that threshold and pretend the world hadn't just lost its center?

John's fingers tightened around hers. "We'll do it together."

Mae looked at him then, really looked. At the way his grief mirrored hers. At the way decades of love had carved itself into the lines around his eyes. They were bound by something deeper than sorrow now—something unspoken and unbreakable.

She took a breath, but didn't move. Neither did he.

Outside, the fog still clung to the world, a thick veil wrapped around the morning. A sliver of sunlight broke through it—faint, hesitant, casting a pale glow over the bed, over their clasped hands, over the space their family would never quite fill the same way again.

Mae didn't know how to leave. John didn't either.

And so, they stayed. Together. In the quiet after.

.

# Chapter 20

# Holding On, Letting Go

A full day had passed, but time had warped—stretching and folding in on itself like grief often does. The sun had risen and fallen, unnoticed behind drawn curtains and unanswered voicemails. Mae drifted through the hours as though underwater, every movement slow, sound muffled, meaning elusive. Her mother was gone, and the world had changed. And though the house looked the same, something fundamental had slipped out of place—like the center beam had cracked.

Friends and neighbors had come, as they always did in this town, to fill the silence with company and food—to show love in the only way they knew how. It was a ritual of presence more than conversation, a quiet custom that said *you are not alone*. Mae hadn't spoken much. She hadn't needed to. The soft hum of voices around her offered their own kind of comfort, even if she wasn't ready to feel it yet.

The house was filled with the low murmur of visitors, condolences blending with the gentle clinking of dishes cleared from the kitchen. The air smelled of warm familiarity—homemade casseroles bubbling beneath layers of cheese, fresh-baked pies cooling on the counter, and the unmistakable scent of slow-cooked brisket mingling with buttery cornbread. The dining table, once the heart of countless family meals, now stood as a display of the town's quiet generosity.

Miss Evelyn from church had brought her famous chicken and dumplings, the thick, creamy broth steaming beneath a golden crust of pillowy dumplings. The Jenkins family, who had lived down the road for as long as Mae could remember, delivered a deep-dish peach cobbler, its cinnamon-sugar crust glistening beneath the kitchen lights. Plates of deviled eggs, green bean casserole with crispy fried onions, and mashed potatoes swirled with pools of melted butter covered every available surface. Someone had even brought a honey-glazed ham, its rich, caramelized exterior sliced into thick, glistening portions.

Mae moved from room to room, her smile automatic, her replies murmured and vague. Her mother was gone, and with her, the anchor that had held everything in place. The world hadn't just changed—it had tilted, and Mae was still searching for steady ground.

She moved through the living room, where Pastor Terry and Dara were speaking quietly with her father. He looked exhausted, his usual sturdy presence weighed down by grief. Every so often, he would squeeze the shoulder of an old friend, nodding solemnly at their words, but Mae knew—just as she felt within herself—that there were no words that could truly soften the loss.

Neighbors and longtime friends filled the room, their faces etched with a shared sorrow. Mrs. Reynolds, who used to babysit Mae when she was little, pressed a warm hand to her cheek, her eyes filled with unshed tears. "Your mama was one of the best, sweetheart," she murmured, giving Mae's hand a squeeze.

Across the room, Mr. Callahan, her father's fishing buddy, stood with his hat in his hands, nodding solemnly as he exchanged memories with a few men from the church. Jenny hovered nearby, keeping a watchful eye on Mae, ready to step in at a moment's notice. Grant had stationed himself near the front door, greeting guests and directing the flow of food with a quiet nod. Crystal lingered near the staircase, her posture uncertain as she took in the sea of familiar faces. When she caught Mae's gaze, she gave her a small, understanding nod.

Mae appreciated it—Crystal had only just begun to truly know Sandy, but in this moment, words weren't needed. There was an unspoken understanding between them—some losses carved spaces in the heart that could never be filled, only carried.

Mae inhaled deeply, the scent of familiar foods and floor polish mingling in her lungs. This was love, she knew—the casseroles, the folded napkins, the soft murmurs—but it all felt like it belonged to someone else's life. Even surrounded by people, Mae couldn't shake the sense that she was orbiting the grief, not standing in it.

Jenny appeared at her side, slipping a warm hand around her arm. "Hey," she said softly. "You've barely eaten anything. Let me fix you a plate."

Mae shook her head, swallowing against the lump in her throat. "I'm not hungry."

Jenny frowned but didn't push. "Then let me take care of the people in here. You go sit with your dad for a bit. You shouldn't have to keep playing hostess."

Mae exhaled, the weight of the room pressing against her ribs. "I don't know what to do with myself, Jenny. Everyone's here, being kind, but it doesn't feel real. I feel like I'm in some sort of dream—detached, like nothing is real anymore."

Jenny's grip tightened. "That's why I'm staying. You don't have to go through this alone."

Mae blinked, her throat thickening. "I know you have to get back to work soon."

Jenny scoffed. "Work can wait. You need me, so I'm here. End of discussion."

Mae let out a shaky breath, the kind that trembled its way out of her chest. "You're such a good friend."

Jenny gave her arm one last squeeze before slipping away into the living room, her presence leaving a soft echo of comfort behind.

The afternoon stretched on, visitors coming and going like the tide—quiet voices, gentle hugs, plates passed, stories shared in soft, broken tones. Eventually, the house began to still, the rhythm of mourning settling into something quieter, something close to calm.

Mae sat at the kitchen table, her fingers tracing a pattern in the condensation of her untouched glass of iced tea. The hum of conversation had faded to the occasional murmur from the other room. For the first time all day, she let herself be still.

She didn't notice Sally enter until the older woman sat down beside her with a soft exhale and a mug of coffee cradled between her hands. Mae looked up, surprised. Sally gave her a warm, familiar smile—the kind that always made Mae feel twelve again, tucked into a booth at the diner with her mom, listening to them laugh over stories she only half understood.

"I've been watching you," Sally said gently, her eyes kind but steady. "Your mama would've swatted me for waiting this long to sit down."

Mae gave a tired laugh. "I keep thinking about all the things I didn't say. The things I didn't ask. I was always... talking. Always needing something."

Sally nodded slowly, setting her mug down with a soft clink. "That's what mamas are for, sweetheart. To be leaned on. And your mama loved being leaned on. She'd call me after y'all talked, you know. Tell me how proud she was of you—even when you drove her a little crazy." She smiled. "Especially when you drove her a little crazy."

Mae's eyes filled unexpectedly. "I just—I wish I'd known her better. Asked her about her life. What she wanted. What she dreamed about before she was a mom."

Sally reached across the table, covering Mae's hand with her own. "Mae, your mama didn't need you to ask all those things to feel seen. You were her dream. And she knew you loved her—every time you picked up the phone, every story you told her, every time you walked through that door. Don't you carry that guilt around like a souvenir. She wouldn't want that for you."

Mae let that settle in the space between them. It was the first thing all day that didn't feel heavy.

They sat like that for a while, not speaking, just breathing in the quiet that followed the storm. Around them, the house began to soften—voices lowering, chairs scraping gently against hardwood, the clatter of dishes growing more distant as the rhythm of the day slowed.

As the crowd began to thin and the steady hum of conversation quieted, Grant leaned against the archway leading into the dining area, watching the room with quiet thoughtfulness. His gaze settled on Crystal, who had barely spoken all afternoon.

He touched her elbow gently, drawing her attention. "Hey," he murmured, leaning in slightly, "I was thinking... if you're ready, I can drive you back to Austin. Give Mae and her dad some space."

Crystal hesitated, her fingers brushing over the rim of her untouched cup of coffee. She cast a glance toward John, who sat at the kitchen table with Pastor Terry, his posture heavy with grief. Then toward Mae, who stood near the fireplace, absently straightening a framed family photo as if grounding herself in the past could steady the present.

Grant was right. This wasn't her home. It never had been. And yet, leaving felt harder than she expected.

Taking a slow breath, Crystal gave a small nod. "Yeah. That's probably for the best."

Grant offered a reassuring smile. "I'll go pack up the truck. Take your time."

She watched as he disappeared down the hall before finally turning to Mae. Their eyes met. There was no lingering tension between them. Just understanding.

Mae approached first, hesitating for only a moment before reaching out. "Thank you, Crystal. For everything."

A soft, bittersweet smile touched Crystal's lips. "Take care of yourself, Mae. And your dad."

Jenny appeared at Mae's side, arms crossed but her expression softer than usual. "You're good at what you do, Crystal," she admitted. "Don't let anyone ever make you feel otherwise."

A flicker of emotion passed over Crystal's face before she nodded, accepting the words for what they were. "Thanks, Jenny. That actually means a lot."

John stood from the table then, approaching them with quiet strength. "You were here for us when we needed you," he said, his voice steady despite the weight of loss in his eyes. "That's something we won't forget."

Crystal swallowed hard and nodded. "It was an honor."

A moment later, Grant reappeared, bags in hand, his truck keys dangling from his fingers. "Ready?"

Crystal glanced back one last time. A look passed between her and Mae—a silent acknowledgment of everything that had changed, of the paths they had both found themselves on. Then she squared her shoulders, exhaled, and followed Grant out the door.

Mae stood in the quiet aftermath, the house now feeling emptier than before. But as she turned back toward her father and Jenny, something about the moment felt right. Like a necessary shift, an inevitable turning of the page. John returned to the living room, receiving a firm handshake and a hand on the shoulder from Mr. Callahan as he said his goodbye's for the night.

Jenny noticed Mae's look on her face, like a lost puppy not knowing where to turn or what to do next, lost in her own home and on the brink of breaking down altogether. Jenny slipped her arm through Mae's, guiding her gently toward the front door.

"Come on, let's grab some fresh air," Jenny said, her voice soft but firm. Mae let herself be led, barely aware of her movements, until they stepped onto the porch. The air was thick with the scent of damp earth and honeydew, the quiet hum of crickets filling the empty spaces between them. They settled onto the porch swing, the wooden slats creaking slightly beneath their weight. Jenny gave Mae's hand a quick squeeze, then turned her gaze toward the driveway as the low, familiar rumble of an approaching engine filled the night air.

Jim's 1967 Ford F-100 rolled up slow, its headlights cutting through the dim evening haze. He parked, killed the engine, and stepped out, his boots scuffing against the gravel. Mae felt a stir in her heart, something unsettling and warm all at once. Jim had always carried himself with a quiet confidence, but tonight there was something softer in his expression, something almost hesitant as he climbed the porch steps.

Jenny caught the shift in the air and stood, stretching her arms. "I'm gonna go check on your dad," she said smoothly, giving Mae a knowing glance before disappearing inside, leaving them alone.

Jim took a few steps closer, then stopped, studying Mae carefully.

"Hey," he said, his voice low, steady.

Mae swallowed hard, her fingers gripping the edge of the swing. "Hey."

She hadn't realized how much she'd missed the sound of his voice—how just his being there untangled something inside her. All the pushing away, all the knots she'd tied herself into... they loosened in the hush between them.

Jim sat down beside her, leaving just enough space for her to breathe, but close enough that his presence felt grounding. He rubbed his palms together, as if searching for the right words. "I don't really know what to say," he admitted after a beat. "Nothing feels like enough."

Mae blinked quickly, staring at the darkened horizon. "There's nothing to say. She's gone, and everyone's been trying to fix it with food and words, but..." She trailed off, pressing her lips together and choking back the tears.

Jim nodded, understanding settling into the lines of his face. "Yeah. I know. When my mom passed, people kept telling me time would help, that it'd get easier. I wanted to believe them, but it just felt... empty, numb."

Mae turned her head, searching his face. "Did it? Get easier?"

Jim exhaled, his gaze drifting to the porch railing. "Not really. It just... changes. One day, you wake up and the weight isn't as crushing. Doesn't mean you don't miss them. Just means you learn to carry it differently."

Jim exhaled slowly, eyes on the horizon. "When my mom died... it felt like the ground went out from under me. People kept saying she was in a better place, but—"

He broke off, his voice catching. He looked away, blinking hard.

"I think that's just something people say because they don't know what else to say."

Mae stayed quiet, her throat tightening.

"I didn't speak at the service," he added after a pause. "I couldn't. I sat there with this speech in my pocket, words I'd practiced a dozen times. But when it came time to stand up... I froze. Felt like nothing I could say would ever be enough."

He rubbed the back of his neck, the memory clearly still raw.

"I carried that regret for a long time. Still do, sometimes. But I've learned—grief doesn't need a perfect performance. It just needs space. Time. Grace."

A tear slipped down Mae's cheek before she could stop it. She swiped at it quickly, but Jim caught her wrist gently, his calloused thumb brushing against her skin. "You don't have to hold it all in, Mae. Not with me."

Her breath hitched. The tenderness in his voice, in his touch, unraveled something inside her. She let out a shaky exhale and leaned into him, just slightly, just enough for his warmth to become something solid. Jim didn't move away. Instead, he wrapped an arm around her, pulling her in, letting her rest against his shoulder. His heartbeat was slow, steady—a quiet promise that she wasn't alone.

They sat together in silence, the night wrapping around them like a quiet embrace. Mae allowed herself to simply exist in the moment, her quiet tears soaking into his shoulder as he held her steady.

# Chapter 21

# Breaking the News

Mae woke to the soft glow of morning light filtering through her curtains, the warmth of her childhood room feeling both comforting and suffocating. For a moment, she let herself pretend it was just another morning, that her mother was downstairs brewing coffee, that life had not unraveled in the span of a few days. But the shrill ring of her phone shattered the illusion.

She reached for it hesitantly, glancing at the caller ID. New York. Her stomach twisted as she sat up, clearing her throat before answering. "Hey, Marc."

"Mae, good morning." Her boss's voice was pleasant, but clipped. "I just wanted to check in, see how you're doing and when you were planning on flying back. This week?"

Mae blinked. No preamble. No concern. Just straight to the point. "Marc... my mom passed away. Two days ago."

Silence. Then, an exhale that sounded more like frustration than sympathy. "I see. I suppose that means you won't be back in the office this week?"

Mae squeezed her eyes shut, gripping the phone tighter. "No, Marc. I won't."

She exhaled, gripping the edge of the comforter. "Marc, I don't know how long I'll need. My dad... he needs me here, and there's still so much to take care of. I have plenty of PTO saved up—"

Marc sighed, and she could almost hear the impatience creeping into his voice. "Mae, I understand, but we can't put everything on hold indefinitely. I'm going to have to reassign your accounts to a junior officer so we can keep things moving. You'll still have a position when you return, but... well, we'll have to discuss what that looks like when the time comes."

As Marc spoke, Mae felt something crack open inside her. A small, treacherous voice whispered that maybe she was done fighting for a place that never fought for her. Maybe she was done trying to prove herself to people who wouldn't even ask how she was holding up.

Mae stilled herself, absorbing his words. "So I'm being demoted."

"No, not demoted," he corrected quickly. "Just reassigned. We'll figure out a place for you when you're ready to come back."

The finality of it settled over her like a weight. After years of giving everything to her job—late nights, early mornings, sacrificing weekends—she was suddenly dispensable.

"Right," she murmured. "I'll let you know."

"Take care, Mae," Marc said, his tone already distant, as if the conversation had run its course.

She hung up, staring at the phone in her hands. Instead of the panic she expected to feel, there was something else—a strange, quiet relief. If her job wasn't concerned about her, why should she be concerned about it?

Pushing the thoughts aside, Mae threw on a sweat shirt and pants and made her way downstairs. The smell of bacon and fresh coffee filled the air, and she found her father at the kitchen table, newspaper folded beside his plate, a steaming mug in front of him.

"Morning, sweetheart," he said softly, his voice low and a little hoarse, like he hadn't used it much yet today. It carried the weight of quiet worry, wrapped in warmth. He offered her a tired but genuine smile. "You sleep okay?"

She poured herself a cup of coffee, adding her ritualistic heap of sugar and vanilla cream and slid into the chair across from him. "Not really." She hesitated, then sighed. "I just got off the phone with Marc. He said they've reassigned my accounts."

John frowned. "Reassigned? What does that mean?"

"It means I still have a job, but not the one I left," she admitted, stirring the cream and sugar into her coffee absentmindedly. "I don't know what I'll be going back to."

Before her father could respond, footsteps padded down the stairs, and Jenny appeared in the doorway, her hair still tousled from sleep. In her oversized pink bunny slippers and a leopard-print silk robe that slipped off one shoulder, she had the look of someone who'd wandered out of a glamorous retro dream and into real life. She had moved into the guest room where

Crystal had been staying—wanting to be closer to Mae during this time and more than a little relieved to escape the drafty loft over the garage.

"Did I hear that right?" Jenny asked, her tone sharper than usual as she slid into the chair beside Mae. "They reassigned your accounts? After everything you've done for that company?"

Mae let out a small, humorless laugh. "Apparently, they couldn't wait for me to come back. Deadlines and all."

Jenny scoffed, crossing her arms. "That's unbelievable. You gave them years of your life, and they couldn't even give you a couple of weeks to grieve?" She shook her head, visibly frustrated. "I know corporate life is brutal, but damn, Mae. That's heartless."

John took a sip of his coffee, his expression thoughtful. "Maybe that's not such a bad thing."

Mae arched a brow. "Losing the job I worked so hard for? How could you say that?"

Her father met her gaze steadily. "Losing something that apparently never really valued you."

Jenny exhaled, leaning back in her chair. "Your dad's got a point. Maybe this is the push you needed."

Mae stared down at her coffee, her mind whirling. She hadn't thought of it that way. But now, with her father's steady wisdom and Jenny's fierce loyalty, the idea of returning to New York felt less like an obligation and more like a choice—one she wasn't sure she wanted to make anymore.

Her father studied her for a moment, then reached over as he stood up with his coffee cup in one hand, giving her a squeeze on the shoulder and whispered in her ear. "Maybe that's not such a bad thing." He continued walking toward the coffee pot to grab a refill.

Before she could respond, his phone buzzed. He glanced at the screen, exhaled, and answered. "John Whitaker."

Mae watched as his face shifted, the strong front he always wore slipping slightly. "Yes, I understand. We'll come by later to finalize everything," he said, his voice steady but strained. "Thank you."

He ended the call and set the phone down, rubbing his fingers over his temple. "That was the funeral home. They had some final questions about the arrangements."

Mae nodded slowly, her chest tightening. "Dad—"

"I think I'm going to take a walk," he interrupted, pushing his chair back. "Get some fresh air."

She didn't try to stop him. Instead, she watched from the window as he made his way down the driveway, his hands shoved deep into his pockets. When he reached the edge of the property, he paused, his shoulders rising and falling in a deep breath. Then, with a slow, weary motion, he wiped at his face.

Mae's heart clenched. Her father, the strongest man she knew, was breaking, and he was doing it alone.

Mae stood by the living room window, arms wrapped around herself, watching as her father disappeared down the road. The weight of everything—the funeral, her job, the uncertain future—pressed heavily on her mind. She exhaled slowly, as if trying to breathe some of it away.

A floorboard creaked behind her. "Mae," Jenny's voice was softer now, missing the fiery indignation it held just minutes ago at the kitchen table.

Mae turned to find her best friend standing right behind her, arms crossed over her chest, her face unreadable.

"Hey," Mae said, her voice weaker than she wanted it to be. "I thought you were still eating."

Jenny scoffed lightly, stepping closer. "Kinda lost my appetite after that conversation." She shook her head. "I still can't believe them. You give them everything, and they just—toss you aside the second it's inconvenient for them?"

Mae let out a short, humorless laugh. "Guess I was more replaceable than I thought."

Jenny's expression darkened, her protective instincts flaring to life again. "That's not true, and you know it. You built that place."

Mae sighed, turning back to the window, tracing patterns in the condensation with her fingertip. "Doesn't change anything."

Jenny was quiet for a beat, then took another step forward. "So... what does your heart say to do?"

Mae swallowed, considering that question for the hundredth time since she'd hung up the phone. "I don't know. I don't even know if I want to go back."

Jenny nodded, as if she had expected that answer. "Maybe that's not such a bad thing."

Mae blinked, glancing at her. "That's exactly what my dad said."

"Smart man," Jenny said with a small smirk. Then, more seriously, "Look, you don't have to decide today. Or tomorrow. Just—give yourself some space, okay?"

Mae met Jenny's eyes, the weight in her chest shifting just a little. "Yeah," she murmured. "Okay."

Jenny nudged Mae's shoulder lightly. "And no matter what you decide, you know I've got your back, right?"

Mae let out a breath, a small smile tugging at the corners of her lips. "Yeah. I know."

And for the first time since she'd answered that phone call, she didn't feel quite so lost. She turned back to the window, her eyes following the bend of the gravel road, quietly hoping her father would return soon.

When he finally did, Mae stepped out to meet him on the porch, moving forward without hesitation and wrapping her arms tightly around him. For a moment, he stood still—then slowly, his arms came around her, holding on just as tightly.

From the doorway, Jenny watched, her eyes glistening with unshed tears. Her hands gripping each other as she pulled them close to her mouth.

"Dad," Mae murmured, her voice thick with emotion. "You don't have to hide this from me."

John exhaled heavily, resting his chin atop her head. "I never wanted you to see me like this, Mae."

Mae pulled back just enough to look up at him. "I'd rather see you like this than not see you at all. We're in this together. Promise me, we're in this together."

John studied her, his weathered face lined with grief and love. Then, finally, he nodded, his expression softening as a tear rolled down his cheek. "You're right. We are."

Mae gave him a watery smile and another embrace before turning toward Jenny, who was sniffling, and quickly wiped at her face. "Come on, get in here" Mae said, extending a hand toward her best friend. "You're family too."

Jenny hesitated for only a second before stepping forward, wrapping her arms around both of them. John huffed a small, amused breath as Jenny squeezed them tightly, her head resting against Mae's shoulder.

"I wasn't going to crash the moment," Jenny sniffed, "but since you invited me..."

Mae let out a soft laugh, and even John chuckled, shaking his head as he held them both close. For a brief moment, the weight of loss lessened, replaced by something steadier—love, support, and the comfort of knowing they weren't facing this alone.

As they stepped inside, Mae felt a quiet shift—not just in the air between them, but deep in her own center. Grief was still present, heavy and unrelenting, but so was purpose. She wasn't just a daughter in mourning; she was a steady hand for her father now, a tether. But she needed him too—needed his steadiness, his quiet strength, the way he made space for her without asking for anything in return. And with Jenny nearby—loud, loyal, and unapologetically herself—Mae knew she had backup for whatever came next.

And then there was Jim.

The thought of him lingered—unspoken but steady. She didn't know exactly what they were, or what they might become, but in the blur of the last few days, he had been a constant. Not asking for anything in return. Not offering hollow reassurances—rather, wisdom, stability, an emotional harbor in a tumultuous sea. Just... there. And somehow, that had meant more than words could express.

# Chapter 22

# Preparing for Goodbyes

The porch creaked beneath Mae's bare feet as she stepped outside, a chipped mug of black coffee in one hand, her notebook in the other. Her father was already there, seated in his usual spot on the porch swing, papers spread across the side table in loose piles that threatened to blow away with the next breeze.

"Morning," Mae said quietly.

John nodded. "Barely slept."

"Me neither."

They didn't need to say why. The funeral was tomorrow.

Mae settled into the wicker chair beside him, the one with the fraying armrest. The air was thick with late spring heat, cicadas humming somewhere in the distance. From the yard, the Texas Mountain Laurel was in full bloom, its pendulous clusters of purple flowers hanging heavy on the branches. The sweet, unmistakable scent—like grape Kool-Aid from childhood summers—drifted across the porch in lazy waves, both comforting and strangely surreal. Her notebook rested on her lap, the pages filled with names, times, and to-do lists that seemed to multiply instead of shrink.

"We still need someone to sing," John said, flipping through a wrinkled program from a funeral two years ago. "You reached out to that choir lady?"

Mae nodded. "She's out of town. Visiting grandkids in Oklahoma."

"What about the Thompson boy? He sang at Ethel's service," John offered, flipping through a dog-eared list of names.

Mae's head snapped up. "He butchered it. He was flat the entire second verse."

John shot her a look. "Mae."

"I'm serious," she said, too fast, too sharp. "It sounded like he was in pain."

"Holy hell, Mae. He was doing his best. You think you could've done better at nineteen?"

"I'm not the one volunteering to sing at a funeral tomorrow."

The words hung in the humid air, heavier than the heat. Even the cicadas seemed to fall quiet.

John stared at her, eyes narrowed. "You know, I don't remember you being this mean when you were home."

She flinched, her stomach lurching. "That's not—" She caught herself, blew out a shaky breath. "I didn't mean it like that."

"You sure? Because it's hard to tell."

Mae dropped her gaze to the notebook in her lap, her voice suddenly small. "I'm tired. I'm... lashing out. I know it. I just—everything feels like it's spinning."

John didn't say anything for a moment. Then, quietly, "It is."

She nodded, the sting of guilt creeping up her spine. "I'll call the Thompson boy. He deserves the chance."

John exhaled slowly, the edge softening in his voice. "We'll figure it out."

He rubbed his jaw, eyes tired. "It's stress. We're both feeling it."

She nodded, picking at the corner of her notebook. "I just... want this to be right. She deserves that."

They sat in silence for a moment, the kind that stretches between people who love each other but don't know what to say.

"We still have to finalize the program," Mae said eventually, flipping to a checklist. "Order of service. Who's speaking. What music. Flowers are set. Food's covered. Bulletins are still at the printer—they promised pick-up by five."

"Dara's coordinating with the church ladies for reception stuff," John added. "So that's off our plate."

Mae made a quick note. "I emailed the obituary to the paper and posted it online. Pastor Terry's doing the eulogy. You're speaking after?"

John hesitated. "I don't know. Thought I might skip that."

Mae looked up, surprised. "But you said you wanted to."

He stared out past the porch railing, toward the trees that lined the property. "I did. But now that it's here..." He trailed off. "I'm not sure I can get the words out."

Mae swallowed hard. "I can help you write it. Or we could read something together?"

He gave her a look, one part grateful, one part weary. "Maybe."

They lapsed into silence again, the only sound the creak of the swing and the buzz of heat rising from the driveway.

She reached for his hand, and this time, he didn't pull away.

"We're doing the best we can," she said, softer now.

"I know." He exhaled. "And she'd be proud of you. Even if the damn singer is off-key."

Mae laughed through a breath that almost turned into a sob. "Maybe we just play a recording."

He shrugged. "Maybe that's best. Less arguing."

They exchanged a glance—tired, tearful, understanding. A fragile sort of peace settled between them.

"We'll get through tomorrow," John said, voice low.

Mae nodded, gripping his hand tighter. "Together."

The quiet held for a beat longer, until the low rumble of a familiar engine drifted up the driveway. Mae glanced toward the road just as Jim's old Ford truck came into view, kicking up a light trail of dust behind it. Her pulse ticked up, subtle but insistent.

He parked with casual ease, stepping out with that quiet confidence that had always clung to him like cologne and sawdust. In his hands was a brown paper bag, the top folded neatly, the weight of it pulling at the thin paper.

Mae sat up a little straighter, brushing her palms against her jeans.

"Jim," John called, rising from the swing. "What ya got there?"

"Figured y'all hadn't been to the store," Jim said as he made his way up the steps. "It's not much. Smoked bacon, eggs, some cinnamon rolls Miss Sally practically forced on me—and I even threw in some of the first official bags of Rocket Smoked Coffee."

Mae smiled, the flutter in her chest still there—insistent now, but still unnamed.

John clapped Jim on the shoulder, his voice gruff with gratitude. "Appreciate it, son. Can't wait to try some."

Mae met Jim's gaze, something unspoken passing between them. She knew why he was here. Not just for her father. Not just out of obligation. He was here for her, too. She felt herself lean into it, just a little. Not fully, but enough to breathe easier.

Jim shifted the bag in his hands. "Let's get this inside before the cinnamon rolls melt."

John pushed open the screen door, holding it for them. The scent of blooming mountain laurel followed them into the cooler shadows of the house, the slam of the porch door cutting off the outside world.

The kitchen was still dim and quiet, but the familiar creak of footsteps echoed from the hallway. A moment later, Jenny appeared, freshly dressed and hair still damp from her shower. She paused in the threshold between the hallway and the kitchen, taking in the scene—the quiet gathering, the warm hum of conversation, the way Mae seemed lighter than she had in days. With a knowing smile, she stepped forward.

"Smells good in here," Jenny said, sliding into a chair beside Mae. "Hope there's enough for one more."

John chuckled, already unloading the groceries onto the counter. "Always. Grab a plate."

Inside, the kitchen glowed with soft morning light pouring through the window above the sink. The scent of sizzling bacon mingled with the sweet hint of cinnamon sugar and something darker, smokier—an aroma Mae knew instantly. Her eyes flicked toward the coffee pot as it hissed and gurgled. That was Jim's roast. She could smell the faint trace of cherry wood even before the first pour.

Jim moved easily around the kitchen, cracking eggs into a bowl and whisking them one-handed while keeping an eye on the skillet. He looked comfortable, like he'd always belonged in that space—though he hadn't stepped foot in it since high school, as far as she could remember.

Jenny leaned in toward Mae, her voice low and teasing. "If I didn't know better, I'd say someone brought husband energy this morning."

Mae shot her a glare, but couldn't suppress the smile tugging at her lips. "Shut up."

"Not denying it, though."

"Jenny."

"Okay, okay," she whispered, grabbing a cinnamon roll and tearing into it with exaggerated innocence.

Jim placed the bacon on a paper towel-lined plate and nodded toward Mae. "You wanna do the honors?" he asked, motioning to the coffee.

Mae stood, poured the first mug, and took a slow sip. The smoky richness filled her mouth—comforting, smooth and bold, like standing close to a cherry wood filled bonfire in the cool dark. She didn't say anything at first, just closed her eyes and let it settle.

"That good?" Jim asked, eyebrows raised.

Mae opened her eyes and smiled at him. "It tastes like home."

Something shifted in his expression then—something warm and uncertain all at once. But before he could respond, John clapped his hands once.

"Alright. Let's eat before everything gets cold."

They gathered around the table—four people in the quiet aftershock of grief, clinging to the small, ordinary act of breakfast. The plates were mismatched. The bacon was slightly too crisp. Someone had forgotten forks. But none of it mattered.

Mae felt something close to peace settle in the room. Not because everything was fixed. Not because tomorrow would be easy. But because, at this one moment, she was not alone, she was home.

The rest of the day passed in a blur of checklists, phone calls, and quiet teamwork. Jenny helped Mae sift through old photo albums to build a beautiful slide deck video set to music, her sharp eye catching details Mae might've missed through tear-blurred vision. They laughed over childhood photos, cried over prom snapshots, and took turns selecting the perfect background song. In the end, they settled on *When I Get Where I'm Going* by Brad Paisley—a song Mae's mother used to hum when she worked in the garden, soft and wistful. It felt like the only choice.

Jim took care of last minute errands with quiet efficiency, never needing to be asked twice. He picked up the printed programs from the shop, double-checked the seating chart with the church staff, and even called in a favor to secure a last-minute soloist Mae and John could both agree on—a honey-voiced woman from one of the acoustic bands that played Friday nights at Rocket Ribs. She wasn't flashy, didn't oversing—just sang with a kind of worn honesty that felt right.

By the time the sun began to dip behind the trees, the impossible had been done. Everything was ready. The food, the flowers, the seating, the service. Mae sat at the dining table staring at the neat stacks of programs, the USB drive holding the video, the framed photo of her mom they'd chosen for the front of the church—and felt a kind of release she hadn't known she was holding back.

A knot in her chest began to loosen. It wasn't peace, exactly, but it was a quiet exhale. The work was done. The decisions had been made. And now, all that remained was to show up, stand still, and say goodbye.

The house had quieted by evening, the steady stream of visitors finally dwindling as night settled over Twinsdale. Mae sat on the front porch, her arms wrapped around herself, hands tucked into the sleeves of her sweatshirt, as the cool breeze drifted through the trees. The sky was inky black, scattered with stars, and the cicadas hummed their twilight melody through the trees. Somewhere in the back of her mind, steady and inescapable, the truth pulsed quietly: tomorrow was her mother's funeral.

Jim stepped onto the porch, his boots scuffing lightly against the wooden planks. He didn't say anything, just settled into the porch swing beside her, stretching his legs out in front of him. Mae glanced at him out of the corner of her eye, appreciating his presence but unsure if she had the energy to talk.

For a while, they just sat there, the silence between them easy, comfortable. Jim rested his arms on the chair's armrests, staring out into the darkness. Mae exhaled slowly, her fingers twisting in her lap.

"Tomorrow's going to be hard," she finally admitted, her voice barely above a whisper. "I don't know how to do this."

Jim didn't rush to respond. He let the words settle, turning them over in his mind before speaking. "You don't have to know how," he said softly. "You just get through it one moment at a time."

Mae glanced at him, struck by the calm certainty in his voice. There was a weight behind it—a kind of quiet understanding that couldn't be taught.

She'd heard whispers over the years about Jim's time overseas—Special Forces, multiple tours, things nobody talked about out loud. And now, hearing him speak with that kind of grounded stillness, she realized he wasn't just offering comfort. He was speaking from experience.

This wasn't the voice of someone guessing how to get through pain—it was the voice of someone who had carried it, lived inside it, and somehow made it back with grace intact.

Mae swallowed the lump in her throat, nodding slowly. "Everyone's been so kind. The food, the prayers, the support... it's overwhelming. But in a good way, I think."

Jim gave a small smile. "That's what community does. It holds you up when you don't have the strength to stand on your own. And your mama—she built something special here. People loved her. They love you and your dad too."

Mae turned toward him, studying his face in the dim glow of the porch light. "You've done a lot, too. More than I can even put into words. Thank you."

Jim shrugged, glancing down at his hands. "It's nothing. Just... making sure you're okay."

Mae hesitated, then reached beside her chair and pulled a folded piece of paper from a book tucked beneath the armrest.

"I've been writing," she said softly, offering it to him. "Just... things I couldn't say out loud. But once I put them on paper, it started to help. Like maybe I was letting go of a little of the weight."

Jim took the paper gently, unfolding it. He read the first lines aloud, his voice low and steady:

*There's a hush beneath the window*
*Where your laughter used to land*
*Now the morning moves without you*
*Like silence unable to stand*
*Time unspools in aching silence*
*Like a ribbon from your hair*
*I reach for you in quiet corners*
*And find only thinning air*

He paused, his fingers smoothing the edge of the page. "Mae... this is beautiful. It's real. You didn't just write something—you captured something."

Mae's eyes shimmered. "It's just how it felt. I wasn't trying to write anything special."

There was a shift in Jim's expression as he lowered the paper—his steely eyes distant now, shadowed with a solemn kind of remembrance. For a breath, he wasn't sitting on a porch in Texas. He was somewhere else entirely.

"I used to write sometimes," he said, almost too casually. "Not poetry. Just... thoughts. Stuff I needed to get out of my head."

His gaze drifted toward the dark horizon. "It helped. Kind of like leaving breadcrumbs back to yourself."

A quiet beat passed.

"You saw things," Mae said gently.

Jim gave a faint smile, but it didn't reach his eyes. "We've all seen something," he murmured, brushing past the moment like it hadn't slipped out at all. Then he tapped the page in his hand. "But this? This is something worth reading. You've got a real gift, Mae."

She blinked, taken aback by the weight of his words.

"It is special," Jim said again, his voice softer now. He glanced down at the paper once more. "Do you mind if I hang on to this for a bit? I've messed around with the acoustic—nothing serious—but I think your words... they sound like they're meant to be sung."

Mae blinked, surprised. "You play guitar?"

Jim gave a small, almost sheepish chuckle. "A little. I mostly keep it to myself. But this... I don't know, it moved something in me. I'd love to see if I can do it justice."

She hesitated, then nodded. "Okay. I'd like that."

Their eyes met—his, warm and sincere; hers, glassy but soft. The moment stretched, quiet and full. Not romantic, not quite yet—but something more than friendship, something tender and slowly unfolding.

They sat there for a long time, the night stretching around them, until Mae finally leaned her head back against the chair, drawing in a deep breath. Tomorrow would come, and it would be hard. But for now, she let herself find comfort in the quiet, in the steady warmth of Jim beside her, and in the knowledge that somehow, some way, she would get through it.

# Chapter 23

# Farewells and New Beginnings

The morning of Sandy's funeral dawned with an overcast sky, as if even the heavens understood the weight of the day. The church was filled to capacity, every pew occupied by family, friends, and neighbors who had come to pay their respects. The air was thick with quiet murmurs, the occasional sniffle breaking through the hushed reverence.

Mae sat between her father and Jenny, her hands clasped tightly in her lap. She had prepared herself for this, had told herself she would be strong, but as soon as the first hymn began, emotion swelled within her. Beside her, John sat stiffly, his eyes locked on the wooden casket at the front of the church. Mae reached for his hand, squeezing gently, and after a moment, he squeezed back.

The service was beautiful—a testament to the life Sandy Whitaker had lived and the love she had left behind. The church overflowed, with people standing in the aisles and lining the back wall. The scent of fresh lilies filled the sanctuary, mingling with warm candle wax and polished wood. Sunlight filtered through the stained-glass windows, casting soft colors onto the pews, illuminating the bowed heads of those gathered.

After Pastor Terry offered his opening prayer and a few words of welcome to this celebration of Sandy's life, the lights dimmed slightly, and the screen behind the pulpit flickered to life. Mae's heart caught in her throat as the slideshow began—the first image, her mother as a young girl, gap-toothed and grinning beside a lemonade stand, elicited soft chuckles from the crowd.

The pictures rolled on, each one painting a fuller picture of the woman Mae loved: Sandy in her prom dress, laughing with her arms slung around her best friend; Sandy beaming with pride, holding baby Mae in a hospital room filled with flowers; Sandy waving from a church bake sale table; Sandy clapping wildly at Mae's high school graduation.

One photo showed Sandy and John on their wedding day, laughing as they stuffed cake into each other's mouths—frosting smudged across Sandy's cheek, John's tie crooked, both of them radiant. There were candid shots, funny ones—like Sandy in an oversized sunhat, chasing a runaway chicken—and poignant ones, including her seated in the garden, lost in thought, her hands nestled in the soil. Brad Paisley's *When I Get Where I'm Going* played softly behind the images, the lyrics sinking into the hearts of everyone watching. The room filled with soft chuckles and quiet sniffles, but more than anything, it filled with the warmth of remembered love.

The final photo faded into view: Sandy walking down a sun-dappled forest path, her back turned slightly toward the camera, but her face turned back—waving with one hand, her other tucked casually in her jacket pocket. Her smile was wide, unrestrained, lit from within with the sheer joy of being alive. It wasn't a posed smile or one meant for appearances—it was the kind of smile that came from deep laughter, from gratitude, from knowing who she was and loving the life she had built.

The trees arched around her like a cathedral, golden light pouring through the leaves and catching in her silver-streaked hair.

And in that moment, Mae didn't feel like she was losing her mother. She felt like Sandy was simply walking ahead, full of peace and joy, waving her onward—just a little farther down the path.

Mae felt herself cry, really cry, that morning. But with the tears came a quiet smile. Her mother had lived a full life—one of joy, service, mischief, and unwavering love. And the room knew it, too.

One by one, people stood to share stories. An elderly woman from the church choir spoke first, her hands trembling slightly as she clutched the microphone. "When my husband passed last year, Sandy was the first person to knock on my door. She brought me meals, sat with me on the hardest nights, and reminded me that I wasn't alone. She had a way of showing up exactly when you needed her."

A man Mae recognized from the hardware store stood next, removing his hat and clearing his throat. "I lost my job a few years back, and things were rough for a while. I didn't tell many people, but Sandy found out. She made sure my kids had Christmas presents that year, left groceries on my porch, and never once made me feel like it was charity. She just cared—that was Sandy."

More stories followed. A young woman spoke of how Sandy had mentored her through a difficult pregnancy. A teenage boy from the youth group recalled how she had encouraged him to pursue music, even buying him his first guitar when his family couldn't afford one. A mother tearfully recounted how Sandy had spent hours praying with her in the hospital when her daughter was sick.

Mae sat, her heart aching but full. Her mother had been more than just her rock—she had been a guiding light to so many.

When Pastor Terry asked if anyone else would like to speak, Mae's breath caught as she saw Jim rise from his seat. He walked slowly to the front, his usual confidence muted by reverence. In one hand, he held his acoustic guitar; the other briefly rested on the back of the pew for support.

"Mrs. Whitaker—Sandy—was one of the first people who made me feel at home in this town," Jim said, his voice steady but raw. "When I came back and started Rocket Ribs, she was one of my first customers. She used to joke that my ribs were good, but my coleslaw needed work."

A soft chuckle moved through the congregation.

Jim smiled faintly, then cleared his throat. "She had this way of making you want to be better—not just in business, but as a person. She believed in people, in second chances, in lifting others up. And she never let you forget that you were worth something." He paused, eyes briefly landing on Mae. "She raised a daughter with that same strength. And I know she's proud of her."

He shifted his guitar strap over his shoulder and turned slightly toward the side of the sanctuary, where a woman stood—a graceful, honey-voiced singer most in the congregation instantly recognized as one of the musicians from Rocket Ribs' Friday night sets – Carrie McRae.

Jim adjusted the mic, his voice quieter now. "Last night, I sat up trying to find the right song for today. But nothing felt right. Then... I came across something that did." He glanced toward Mae, his voice gentling. "A poem. One that didn't need much—just a melody. It sort of wrote itself after that."

He hesitated, a hand brushing the back of his neck. "Carrie and I rehearsed it this morning. I hope we've had enough time to get it right. And if I mess up... well, forgive me. I just knew this was the right way to honor Sandy."

Mae tilted her head, puzzled—until the first few chords rang out soft and low, and Carrie's voice rose, clear and full of emotion.

*There's a hush beneath the window*

*Where your laughter used to land*
*Now the morning moves without you*
*Like silence unable to stand*

Mae's breath caught. She knew those words. Her hand went to her chest. It was her poem.

*Time unwinds in aching silence*
*Like a ribbon from your hair*
*I reach for you in quiet corners*
*And find only thin air*

She blinked fast, trying to keep her vision from blurring, but it was no use. Jim had read it—really read it. And now here it was, offered aloud in a room full of people, her private grief becoming a shared farewell.

*So this is the quiet after*
*This numbing pain creates no sound*
*The space your laughter once shimmered*
*Is now in pieces on the ground*
*So this is the quiet after*
*Emotions crash, then ebb from shore*
*This is the quiet after*
*Where healing waits behind the door*

A hush had fallen over the sanctuary. Even the faint creak of pews and rustle of tissues had gone still. The song had gathered everyone into its quiet gravity.

*Your words still live in daylight*
*In the steam above my tea*
*In the way I fold a bedsheet*
*In the questions still in me*
*You told me love was legacy*
*That kindness never dies*
*And now your wisdom breathes in silence*
*Like the stars across the sky*

Mae reached for Jenny's hand without looking. She could feel her best friend trembling beside her, crying silently but openly.

*So this is the quiet after*
*Where memory learns to sing*

*Where grief becomes a rhythm*
*And your voice becomes the strings*
*No, you are not gone in echo*
*Not lost in sleep or dream*
*You live within the quiet after*
*Where I still speak your name*
*You will always be with me*
*In the quiet after*

When the last note faded, silence fell over the church—not empty silence, but full. Full of memory, of love, of something too deep for words.

Mae looked at Jim, her heart aching and full all at once. He met her gaze with quiet steadiness.

And in that look, she understood: her grief had been heard, her love honored.

She wasn't alone.

After the graveside service, the town gathered at the church hall for the repast. The air was thick with the aroma of comfort food—fried chicken crisped to perfection, creamy casseroles still warm from the oven, platters of slow-cooked greens, and cornbread golden and fragrant. Pies lined a long folding table, each one made with care—apple, pecan, and Sandy's favorite, banana cream pie, brought by Mrs. Wilkins from two doors down. The hall, usually a place of cheerful fellowship, carried a quieter, more reverent tone today.

Mae moved through the space in a daze, stopping here and there to accept hugs, murmur thanks, and listen to fond recollections of her mother. Everyone had a story, a memory, a moment where Sandy had been their rock. It was overwhelming, but in a way that wrapped around Mae like a soft quilt—painful, but also comforting.

She spotted Jim near the corner of the room, helping to refill pitchers of sweet tea. For a moment, she just watched him—how easily he blended into her world, how quietly he helped without drawing attention.

She walked over, her voice low. "Jim?"

He turned, setting the pitcher down. "Hey. You doing okay?"

Mae nodded, her eyes misty. "I just wanted to say... thank you. For the song. For everything. That was..." She paused, her throat tightening. "It meant more than I can say."

Jim offered a soft smile, his voice just above a whisper. "You already said it. In the poem."

She looked down, then back at him. "Still. Thank you for making it into something... bigger."

He gave a small shrug, humble as ever. "I just followed your lead. This day's about her—and about you. Soak it in. Let people love on you a little."

Mae's lip trembled with a smile. "Trying."

Jim stepped back slightly, his tone easy. "I'm gonna go help clean up out back—looks like they're short on hands. But I'll be around if you need anything."

She nodded. "Okay."

And just like that, he gave her space—not out of distance, but out of deep, quiet understanding.

Crystal and Grant had arrived just before the service, slipping into a pew near the back. Now, as people milled about, Crystal found Mae standing near the dessert table, absentmindedly stirring a cup of coffee.

"Hey," Crystal said softly.

Mae turned, offering a small, tired smile. "Hey."

Crystal hesitated, then glanced down at the coffee in Mae's hands. "How are you holding up?"

Mae exhaled, her shoulders rising and falling with the breath. "I don't know. It feels like I've been on my feet for days, but also like I don't want to sit down because that would mean stopping. And if I stop..." She trailed off, shaking her head.

Crystal nodded in understanding. "I get that. It's like if you keep moving, the weight of it doesn't settle so heavy."

Mae looked at her then, really looked at her. There had been a time, not so long ago, when she wasn't sure they'd ever have a moment like this—where they could stand together and simply be. "Thank you for coming. It means a lot."

Crystal offered a small smile, something softer than Mae had seen from her in weeks. "Your mom was incredible. She was always so kind to me when we were younger, even when I didn't deserve it."

Mae's lips quirked, a sad but knowing smile forming. "That's just who she was. She had a way of seeing the best in people, even when they couldn't see it in themselves."

Crystal swallowed, looking down at her hands before meeting Mae's gaze again. "She'd be really proud of you, you know."

A lump formed in Mae's throat, and she nodded, blinking away the sting behind her eyes. "I hope so."

For a moment, there was silence—not an awkward one, but something comfortable, something healing. Whatever had once been a wedge between them had crumbled, leaving behind nothing but understanding. They had both found what they were looking for, in different ways, and there was peace in that.

Grant approached then, two plates balanced in his hands. "Figured you ladies could use some food before it's all gone. This town sure knows how to cook."

Mae let out a small laugh, shaking her head. "Yeah, they do."

Crystal glanced at Grant before looking back at Mae, a quiet acceptance in her expression. "Eat something, okay? You need to take care of yourself."

Grant stood for a moment, scanning the room, his hands tucked loosely in his pockets. He caught sight of Jim, who had just finished shaking hands with one of the church elders, and made his way over. Jim looked up as Grant approached, nodding in greeting.

"Hell of a turnout," Grant said, glancing around at the packed hall. "Says a lot about your town. About her."

Jim nodded, his expression solemn. "Yeah. Sandy was special. She meant a lot to a lot of people."

Grant paused, then added, "That song... it was beautiful. Hit everyone right in the gut."

Jim gave a small smile and shook his head. "I appreciate that—but the real beauty was in the words. Mae wrote the poem. I just gave it a tune."

Grant's eyebrows lifted, visibly impressed. "No kidding?"

Jim's gaze shifted toward Mae across the room, her head bowed in quiet conversation with a neighbor. "She poured her heart into it. I just helped it sing."

Grant lowered his voice slightly. "Listen, I wanted to talk to you about something. Told a buddy of mine about your place. Daniel Vaughn—writes for

Texas Monthly. He's always on the hunt for good barbecue, and I figured he might want to check your place out."

Jim stilled, blinking at Grant as if trying to process what he had just said. "Wait—Daniel Vaughn? The guy who does the Top 50 list?"

Grant smirked. "One and the same. I mentioned Rocket Ribs & BBQ, told him about your brisket, your ribs... and that little something extra you've been working on."

Jim narrowed his eyes slightly, as if wary of believing too soon. "You serious?"

Grant chuckled, clapping a firm hand on Jim's shoulder. "Dead serious. Don't know when he'll come through, but keep an eye out. Could be big."

Jim ran a hand over the back of his neck, nodding slowly as the weight of Grant's words settled in. He had poured everything into Rocket Ribs & BBQ—his passion, his sweat, the lessons his father had passed down to him. And now, maybe, there was a real chance for it to be recognized in a way he'd never even let himself hope for.

"Dang," Jim finally said, exhaling. "That's... that's huge, man. Appreciate that. More than you know."

Grant grinned. "Figured you wouldn't mind a shot at the big leagues. Just be ready when he comes knocking. Those guys don't mess around."

Jim let out a low chuckle, shaking his head. "Yeah. I'll be ready."

Grant smirked. "Good. Because something tells me you're about to be a lot busier than you planned."

Jim just smiled, a flicker of something new—some-thing hopeful—sparking in his eyes.

As the evening wound down, the hall began to empty. The warmth of the gathering gave way to the inevitable goodbyes, the quiet hum of voices mingling with the distant sound of crickets just outside the open windows. The overhead lights cast a soft glow over the remaining guests, illuminating the bittersweet smiles and lingering embraces that came with the close of a long and emotional day.

Mae stood near the doorway, wrapping her arms around herself as she watched people trickle out in small groups, exchanging quiet words and heartfelt goodbyes. The weight of exhaustion settled over her, but underneath it, there was something else—a quiet understanding that life, somehow, was still moving forward.

Grant and Crystal approached her, their expressions softer than usual. Grant held his car keys loosely in one hand, his other stuffed into the pocket of his blazer. "Time to head back to Austin," he said, his voice easy but carrying an underlying sincerity.

Crystal shifted beside him, meeting Mae's gaze with something almost like gratitude. "You doing okay?" she asked, though they both knew the answer was layered.

Mae nodded, offering a tired but genuine smile. "I will be."

Crystal gave her a knowing look, then glanced across the room to where Jim stood talking quietly with Jenny near the dessert table. Her lips twitched upward. "Don't overthink it too much."

Mae let out a soft laugh, shaking her head. "No promises. Overthinking is what I do best."

Grant stepped forward, pulling Mae into a firm hug. "Take care of yourself," he murmured. "And don't be a stranger. You've got people in Austin who'd be happy to see you."

Mae squeezed his arm, appreciating the sentiment more than she could express. "Thanks, Grant. For everything."

Crystal followed with her own embrace, lingering just long enough for Mae to feel the unspoken understanding between them. They had started out as something close to adversaries, but now? Now, they were just two people who had made peace with where life had led them.

As Grant and Crystal walked toward the door, Mae watched them go, their silhouettes framed against the deep golden hue of the Texas evening. The sound of their car doors opening and shutting drifted in through the quiet hall.

Mae stood still, letting the silence settle around her, listening to the soft clatter of plates being stacked, chairs scraped gently across the floor.

She turned and caught sight of Jim at the far end of the hall, folding tables and lining up chairs with quiet focus. No spotlight, no need for thanks—just steady, thoughtful presence. The same presence that had carried her through the last few days.

There was something grounding about the sight of him like that—part reverent, part real. As if the weight of the day hadn't shaken him, only made him steadier.

A chapter had closed, but another was just begin-ning. She wasn't sure what came next—but watching Jim in that moment, she felt the possibility of something more. Something honest. Something hers.

Mae took a breath and let it fill her. She was ready to turn the page.

Click here to listen to the song "The Quiet After" by Carrie McRae

# Chapter 24

# A Call for Change

The morning sun cast a warm glow over the fields as Mae and Jenny loaded the last of Jenny's bags into the trunk. The air was crisp, carrying the faint scent of honeysuckle and earth—a scent that felt rooted and old, unlike the brash city air Jenny would be returning to. The hum of cicadas blended with the distant call of a mourning dove, filling the space between them with a quiet, familiar rhythm.

John stood on the porch, a steaming mug of coffee in one hand, his other shielding his eyes as he watched the women move around the car. He looked only half awake—his flannel shirt misbuttoned and hair still sleep-tousled—but his gaze was steady and fond.

"You sure you don't need me to ride with you to the airport?" he called, voice gravelly.

Jenny shut the trunk and turned with a grin. "As tempting as it is to get a front-row seat to your backseat driving, I think Mae and I can manage."

John snorted. "Suit yourself."

Jenny walked up to him and opened her arms wide. "C'mere, you old softie. You're not getting out of this goodbye without a hug."

He chuckled but returned it without hesitation, patting her back with a little more pressure than usual. "Thanks for everything, Jenny. You've been an anchor for Mae through all this."

Jenny pulled back, eyes bright. "Wouldn't have been anywhere else. Just make sure you eat something green once in a while. And maybe drink a glass of water that isn't brewed with beans, once in a while."

John shook his head, smirking. "If water tasted like ribs, I'd be a damn health guru by now."

Jenny winked. "If only..."

They loaded into the car and started down the gravel driveway, the house growing smaller behind them, its porch now empty except for the lingering warmth of their time there. For a while, neither of them spoke, letting the early light and open road fill the space.

Eventually, conversation surfaced, soft and familiar. They talked about Jenny's next big case, office gossip, and how nothing in New York would ever come close to the smoky brisket from Rocket Ribs.

Then the playlist shifted.

The opening beat of Man! I Feel Like a Woman! by Shania Twain burst through the speakers, bold and unmistakable.

Jenny gasped like she'd just spotted a celebrity, then flung both hands up midair like she was directing traffic.

"Hold up. No talking. This is sacred."

She tapped an invisible DJ table, lifted her arm like she was cueing a spotlight, and struck a pose full of attitude.

Mae glanced over. "Oh no..."

Jenny didn't answer. She was already in the moment. Shoulders back. Chin up. Full of confidence. She mouthed along to the opening, letting the rhythm take over, then broke into exaggerated air guitar, strumming like she was headlining her own arena tour.

Mae tried to hold it together. She failed.

"Oh, good grief," she muttered, rolling her eyes, but smiling and giggling despite herself.

Jenny spun toward her, eyes wide now, fully locked in. She leaned across the console and thrust an invisible microphone inches from Mae's face, eyebrows raised in expectation.

"Don't you dare leave me hanging," she said, half-laughing, half-commanding.

Mae shook her head. "Absolutely not."

Jenny doubled down, performing harder now, like refusal only fueled her.

And that was it.

Mae cracked.

She joined in, laughing, drumming the steering wheel, giving in to the moment she couldn't resist. Whatever dignity remained disappeared somewhere between the beat and Jenny's commitment to the bit.

Within seconds, they were both all in.

Windows down. Voices loud. Confidence completely unearned.

They didn't need the words. They knew the feeling.

Freedom. Noise. A kind of joy that didn't ask permission.

Jenny tossed her hair like she was onstage at the Grand Ole Opry. Mae pounded the steering wheel in rhythm, laughing so hard at one point she nearly missed the exit.

They kept singing, hopping through the playlist like they were DJing their own private concert. Every few songs, one of them would shout, "Oh! This one! The B-52's!" and crank the volume. There were throwback anthems from college parties, road trip staples, and a few shameless guilty pleasures they knew every word to.

Mae leaned into it, letting the music loosen something in her that had been locked up for weeks. Jenny played air drums on the dashboard, and at one point even tried to harmonize with Adele—badly—which only made them laugh harder.

They ebbed in and out of the fun. When the songs faded to background noise, conversation would drift in—easy, honest, never forced. They talked about work, about New York, about the awkwardness of being between two lives. Jenny didn't press, just listened. Every now and then she'd offer a nudge.

"Look, you don't have to move back to Texas," she said, cracking open a bottled water. "But you should at least figure out what *you* want—not what anyone else expects."

Mae nodded, staring out the window at the flat stretch of highway, the trees blurring by. "I don't know what that is yet."

"Good. That's your starting point."

More music followed. They sang loud. They got quiet. They shared a bag of peanut M&M's that Jenny found in her purse and debated whether stopping for In and Out Burger once they got to Austin was worth the detour.

The miles rolled by like that—full of rhythm and memory and the kind of laughter that didn't erase the hard stuff, just made space around it.

By the time Austin's skyline came into view, their voices were a little hoarse, their cheeks sore from smiling, and Mae felt... not fixed, but steadier.

And for now, that was enough.

Jenny didn't press, but as they neared the airport, she turned down the radio and glanced over.

"You don't have to have answers yet," she said gently. "But whatever's pulling at you? Don't ignore it."

Mae nodded, eyes fixed on the road. "I'm still going back. At least for now."

Jenny gave a knowing smile. "Of course. I'll see you as soon as you're back—and your inbox has swallowed you whole."

They pulled into the terminal lane, and Mae shifted the car into park. Without waiting, Jenny unbuckled her seatbelt and flung the door open like a woman making a grand entrance.

"Alright, Austin-Bergstrom," she declared as she stepped out, hands on her hips like she was about to strut a runway. "Prepare yourself."

Mae rolled her eyes but couldn't help smiling as she got out, circling to the back to grab Jenny's bag.

Jenny intercepted her halfway and threw her arms wide. "Nope. No quick goodbye. I want the full dramatic farewell."

Mae laughed and opened her arms. Jenny pulled her into a tight, theatrical hug—complete with a dramatic sigh and a faux whisper, "Promise me you'll write every day."

Mae snorted, looking at Jenny with oozing sarcasm. "You'll be lucky if I answer your texts."

Jenny pulled back and looked at her with exaggerated seriousness, then softened. "You're stronger than you think. And whatever you decide—you've got this."

Mae's smile wobbled, the humor giving way to something more tender. "Thanks, Jenny. For everything."

Jenny slung her carry-on over her shoulder like a seasoned traveler—a bright floral tote with oversized gold zippers and a neon pink tassel swinging from the strap—and gave a mock salute. "I'll be expecting a life update within the week. Preferably over wine. Or queso."

"Wine's more likely."

"Atta girl."

She blew a kiss over her shoulder as she turned, her wheeled suitcase trailing behind her like a loyal sidekick. It was leopard print, naturally, with a sparkly luggage tag shaped like a high heel. The wheels squeaked faintly as she strutted toward the terminal, unbothered.

With one final wink, she disappeared into the sliding doors, swallowed by the airport crowd in typical Jenny fashion—like she belonged to every room she entered, and none of them at all.

Mae stood for a moment, arms crossed, watching the doors close behind her best friend. And just like that, the quiet settled in again.

She wasn't alone—not really—but the silence felt louder now. The world had gone still again.

And this time, it was up to her to decide what came next.

As she pulled out of the airport parking lot, the open road stretched before her, full of possibility and uncertainty. And maybe, just maybe, she was finally ready to face it.

Instead of heading straight back to Twinsdale, Mae decided to stop for lunch at Bouldin Creek Cafe, a beloved vegetarian eatery in Austin known for its vibrant atmosphere and delicious plant-based dishes. The cafe has grown from a small coffeehouse into a community hub that emphasizes sustainability and local art.

As she stepped inside, the rich aroma of freshly brewed coffee and spices enveloped her. The interior was a tapestry of colorful murals and eclectic decor, reflecting the artistic spirit of the city. Patrons chatted animatedly at mismatched tables, and the hum of the espresso machine blended seamlessly with the indie music playing softly in the background.

Scanning the room, Mae's eyes landed on a familiar figure at the counter—Grant. He was engrossed in conversation with the barista, his easygoing demeanor evident even from a distance. A smile tugged at the corners of her mouth as she made her way over, the warmth of the cafe seeping into her bones.

Grant noticed Mae at the same time and grinned. "Well, look who it is."

Mae smirked, sliding onto the stool beside him. "Didn't expect to run into you here."

Grant sipped his coffee, setting the mug down with a satisfied sigh. "Had some business in town. Figured I'd grab some lunch before heading back." He studied her, his gaze steady but not prying. "How you holding up kid?"

Mae exhaled, her fingers tracing the rim of the menu in front of her. "Getting through it. One day at a time."

Grant nodded in understanding, then signaled the barista. "Well, let's make today a good one. Lunch is on me."

They placed their orders—Mae choosing a hearty breakfast taco and a side of fruit, while Grant opted for the cafe's renowned tofu scramble. As they waited for their food, conversation drifted naturally. Grant told her about his company's latest projects, a mix of oil investments and real estate ventures, and Mae found herself genuinely interested. It had been a while since she'd talked business with someone who wasn't rushing through a call between meetings.

But when Grant turned the topic to her, Mae hesitated. She hadn't really said it out loud yet—not to anyone besides Jenny. She hadn't put words to the uncertainty that had been gnawing at her since her boss reassigned her accounts.

"So what's next for you?" Grant asked, leaning back in his chair, stirring the last of his coffee.

Mae let out a breath, curling her hands around her mug. "I don't know. I mean, I know I'm not ready to leave Twinsdale. Not yet. And going back to my old job? It doesn't feel right anymore."

Grant lifted an eyebrow. "I thought you liked your job. Something in publishing, right?"

"Technically," Mae said, with a wry half-smile. "I was the head of marketing for a lifestyle imprint. Think polished Instagram campaigns, holiday gift guides, influencer tie-ins... all the usual glitz."

Grant nodded, listening.

"But when I asked to extend my leave after Mom passed," she continued, "the tone shifted. Passive-aggressive emails. Hints at 'realignment.' And when I came back from the funeral, there was a meeting on my calendar titled *Reimagining Your Role*." She let out a short, bitter laugh. "Grief, it turns out, doesn't play well with quarterly performance goals."

Grant winced. "That's rough."

"It made me realize how replaceable I was to them," Mae said quietly. "And how misplaced my loyalty was."

He was quiet for a beat. Then: "Well, that's their loss."

She looked up, surprised by the warmth in his tone.

"You know, my company contracts out a lot of our marketing work," Grant said. "We've been looking for someone who knows how to tell a real story—something with heart. Most of the firms we've used are flashy but shallow. You, though..." He paused. "You wrote about your mom in a way that made people cry and then want to bake something. That's a gift."

Mae blinked. "Are you offering me a job?"

"I'm offering you a conversation," he said with a grin. "But yes—if you're interested, I can set it up. It would be remote, freelance stuff to start. Flexible schedule. No soul-sucking meetings. You'd have the freedom to build something your own way."

She leaned back, considering. "That sounds... amazing."

"And real," he added. "Not a maybe. You'd start with a paid project—test the waters. If it's a fit, we expand from there."

Mae's heart picked up. She sat back in her chair, feeling something unfamiliar rush through her—not panic or fear, but possibility. Spontaneity. Adrenaline. The kind she hadn't felt since... college. When decisions were made on gut instinct and late-night pizza, not spreadsheets and survival.

And surprisingly, it felt good. Right. Freeing.

"Let me make a call first," she said looking at Grant with a devilish look and a grin, her voice lighter than usual.

Grant nodded, understanding. "I'll be right here."

She stepped outside the café, the sun warming her shoulders as she took out her phone. For a moment, she just stood there, watching a breeze rustle the flags strung across Main Street. The morning light hit the windows just right, casting soft reflections over the storefronts. She could see Grant through the glass, still sipping his coffee, giving her space but watching with quiet encouragement.

Mae smiled to herself. Maybe she didn't need to have it all figured out. Maybe this moment—was enough.

She pulled up the contact and stared at Marc's name on the screen.

Then she tapped it.

The phone rang twice.

"Mae," Marc answered, brisk and clipped. "I hope you're calling with good news."

She exhaled, steadying her voice. "I'm not coming back."

Silence. She could imagine him blinking, reaching for his stress ball, already mapping out how to reassign her accounts.

"Mae—" he started, but she cut in, calm and clear.

"I'm grateful for the experience, but I've made my decision. I'll send my formal resignation by the end of the day."

Another beat of silence.

"Is this about the reorganization?"

"It's about the fact that I've changed," she said simply.

Before he could respond, she added, "Take care, Marc," and ended the call.

When she turned to go back inside, Grant was still there, watching her through the window. She raised her brows in a silent *well, that's done*, and he lifted his coffee in a salute.

She felt the smile spread across her face before she realized it was happening.

It wasn't freedom yet—not fully—but it was the first step. And it felt damn good.

Home.

The word felt right. It settled into her bones, warm and certain. She wasn't looking back.

She was going home.

# Chapter 25

# The Best is Yet to Come

The late afternoon sunbathed the rolling fields in gold, stretching long shadows across the weathered wood of Rocket Ribs & BBQ's front porch. The Texas sky, vast and endless, seemed to hum with the promise of something unspoken. The warm breeze carried with it the scent of post oak smoke and wildflowers, wrapping around Mae like a familiar embrace. It was a scent she had once associated with fleeting summers and trips to Lockhart. Now, it smelled like home.

The drive back from Austin had passed in a haze of sunlit roads and shifting thoughts. Mae kept replaying the what just happened on a loop—Grant's offer, the call to Marc. How quickly everything had tilted. How, in the span of one lunch, her life had quietly realigned itself.

Could she really do this?

Was she really doing this?

There were moments, especially on the quiet stretches of highway, when doubt slipped in—thin and sharp as a thorn. Was she crazy for walking away from stability? From a career she'd built brick by brick? She had no five-year plan, no polished roadmap. Just a project, a promise, and a gut feeling.

But then she'd think of that phone call. The way her voice had sounded—steady, clear, unmistakably hers. The silence on Marc's end as he realized she wasn't bluffing. That strange, giddy rush afterward, like she'd just jumped off a cliff and found herself plunging into a cool, crisp mountain lake.

She hadn't expected it to feel like freedom.

And even now, as uncertainty fluttered within her, it was edged with something else. Relief. Pride. A sense of rightness that she couldn't explain, only feel.

As she'd rounded the last bend toward town, the radio had kicked over to David Lee Murphy's *"Everything's Gonna Be Alright"*—an easy, familiar beat she hadn't realized she needed until it filled the cab like a warm breeze.

She smiled in spite of herself, fingers tapping the steering wheel as the chorus drifted through the speakers. It wasn't profound. It wasn't poetry. But it was something else—reassurance. The kind that slipped in sideways when your heart wasn't looking.

Everything's gonna be alright, don't go hittin' that panic button...

The lyrics floated in the background as the old oak trees lining Main Street came into view, swaying gently in the breeze. And for the first time in a long time, Mae didn't reach for the what-ifs or the worst-case scenarios.

She just listened. And let herself believe it.

By the time she reached the front of Rocket Ribs, the song had faded, but the feeling lingered—quiet assurance humming to her core. She hadn't planned to stop. She'd meant to go straight home, let the weight of the day melt into the porch swing beside her dad. But her hands had turned the wheel almost on their own, guiding her here like muscle memory.

Now she stood at the wooden railing, watching. Jim moved with quiet precision near the smoker, sleeves rolled up, the muscles in his forearms flexing as he tended the slow-burning embers. His rhythm was steady, almost meditative, as though the fire answered only to him. Smoke curled lazily into the sky, a swirl of post oak and cherry wood mingling with the fading warmth of the day.

She could still remember the way she had stood in this very spot, arms crossed, challenging him with a smirk that masked her own uncertainty.

And now—now she stood here again, changed.

She wasn't that woman anymore.

The restless ache that had once driven her to New York, the need to prove herself in a world that measured worth in deadlines and high-rise offices, had faded. In its place was something steadier, something deeper. She had spent so long running toward an idea of success, only to realize that home—real, lasting, unshakable home—had been here all along.

Jim glanced up then, his eyes finding hers through the haze of smoke curling from the pit. For a moment, neither of them spoke. The late afternoon light caught the golden flecks in his brown eyes, making them look warmer, softer. He wiped his hands on a rag, stepping closer, his expression unreadable. But there was something in his gaze—something knowing, something patient, something that made Mae feel like she had been walking toward this moment for a long time.

"You hungry?" he asked, his voice a low rumble, rough from the smoke and long hours of work.

Mae hesitated, then smiled, the corners of her lips curving up as she met his gaze. "Yeah. I think I am."

She wasn't just talking about food.

Jim studied her for a beat, then smirked, that slow, easy grin of his that had always made her stomach flip. "Twice in one week, Whitaker? People are gonna start talking."

Mae folded her arms across her chest, tilting her head as she leaned against the railing, flashing a devilish grin. "Let them."

Jim let out a quiet chuckle, but his amusement didn't quite reach his eyes. He stepped closer, close enough that she could smell the smoke clinging to his shirt, the faint trace of the smoke mixing with something inherently him. The teasing in his expression faded, replaced by something quieter, something searching.

"How you holding up?" he asked.

Mae exhaled, her fingers trailing idly along the wooden railing. "Better." She paused, glancing at the familiar sight of Rocket Ribs & BBQ, the place that had somehow become her anchor. "But being here... it helps."

Jim nodded, his gaze steady. "When you heading home to New York?"

Mae hesitated, looking past him, past the pit and the restaurant, toward the open fields that stretched beyond the road. The answer had once been so clear, so simple. New York had been her home. Her career. Her future.

But now, the idea of leaving felt foreign. Wrong.

"I am home," she said, the certainty in her voice surprising even herself. "I am home."

Something flickered across Jim's face—relief, maybe, or something deeper. He reached for her hand, his fingers rough and calloused from years of hard work. But his touch was gentle, grounding. His thumb brushed lightly over the back of her hand, sending warmth spiraling through to her core.

"Good," he murmured. "I was hoping you'd say that."

A quiet understanding passed between them, a thread weaving something unseen but undeniable. Mae had spent so much of her life running, chasing a version of success that had never quite fit. But standing here, with Jim's steady hand wrapped around hers, she realized she wasn't lost anymore. She wasn't searching for something else.

She had already found it.

Jim cleared his throat, breaking the silence with a crooked smile. "So, you gonna come inside and eat, or are you just here to stare at me while I work?"

Mae rolled her eyes but let him tug her toward the door, her laughter mixing with the hum of the Texas evening and the George Strait song playing in the background. And as they stepped inside, she realized she was exactly where she was meant to be.

# Chapter 26

# The Finale

The late afternoon light stretched over the Texas horizon, painting the sky in streaks of amber and violet as dusk was about to set in. Mae pulled into the gravel lot of Rocket Ribs & BBQ, the crunch beneath her tires grounding her as she took a deep breath. This place had become more than just a restaurant—it was a symbol of everything she had come back to. And everything she had finally chosen to stay for.

It had been a few weeks since she made the call that quietly rerouted the rest of her life. Jenny had taken the news with her usual flair—shocked at first, then overwhelmingly supportive. "You're what? Wait—are we crying or celebrating? Because I've got champagne *and* tissues," she'd said, already opening the bottle before Mae finished the sentence.

Mae had flown back to New York a few days later, just long enough to pack up the life she no longer needed. She spent one long weekend in her apartment, sorting through memories and deciding what came with her and what stayed behind. A moving company had been scheduled in advance, and by the time she locked the door for the final time, her boxes were already en route to Twinsdale—labeled, stacked, and on their way to a new chapter.

The apartment felt smaller than she remembered—like her grief had expanded the walls and now she didn't quite fit anymore. She gave away most of the big stuff: the vintage bar cart Jenny had always admired, the mirror that had survived three moves, the antique leather chair she barely used. Jenny came over to help pack and walked away with half her wardrobe and a bottle of overpriced olive oil.

Packing her desk at work had been oddly cathartic. She took her time, carefully peeling off old sticky notes, tucking away the few personal photos she'd let herself keep on display. When she carried her box of personal items to the elevator, she didn't feel bitterness—only clarity. Her body may have been there, but her heart was somewhere else. Walking out for the last time felt like closing a chapter she'd been skimming for too long.

She flew back into Austin the next day, landing to warm sun and the subtle scent of sage in the air. She had been driving a rental car ever since she flew into Dallas the day after her father's call. Before heading to New York, she'd returned it—along with the version of herself who had arrived on autopilot, bracing for loss.

Now, as she stepped onto the curb at the Austin airport, a sharply dressed woman holding a Hillside Audi sign waved her down with a grin.

"Mae Whitaker?" the woman asked, opening the back door of a sleek black sedan.

"That's me," Mae said, smiling as she slid inside.

Fifteen minutes later, she was sitting behind the wheel of her new Audi A5 convertible—pre-owned but gleaming, top down and already dusted with sunshine. It wasn't overly flashy—it was freedom. She merged onto the highway with the wind in her hair and the wide Texas sky overhead, heading home.

Back in Twinsdale, life began to take a shape that felt... hers.

Her dad had grinned wide when she told him she wasn't going back. "You know the guest room's yours as long as you want it," he'd said, handing her a slice of pie. "Only rent I'll charge is helping me refill the coffee pot."

Grant had made good on his offer, and Mae had officially signed on for her first freelance project. It wasn't glamorous, but it was meaningful—and it was hers. She cleared out a corner of the guest room for a desk, lit a candle every morning, and let herself dream on paper again.

And then there was Jim.

It wasn't fast. It wasn't loud. But it was steady.

At first, he'd started texting her good morning. Bringing her a coffee when he passed her dad's house. Text messages turned into porch visits. Porch visits turned into late-night drives.

One night, after closing up the restaurant, he'd sat with her on the tailgate of his truck and talked about his mom for the first time. She hadn't said much—just listened. And that seemed to be enough.

She'd told him about the way her grief came in waves—less frequent now, but still unexpected. And in the quiet that followed, they simply existed together—no pressure, no performance, just presence.

It was slow. It was safe. It was unfolding in its own time.

Earlier that afternoon, Jim had called her, his voice somewhere between excitement and hesitation.

"Can you come by?" he'd asked. "There's something I want to open with you."

Now, as she stepped out of her convertible and smoothed her hands over her jeans, Mae felt her heart beat just a little faster—not from nerves, but from something closer to anticipation.

Whatever this was, whatever came next... she was ready to open it too.

Now, standing outside, she smoothed the hem of her blouse and made her way up the wooden steps of the patio. Jim stood near the fire pit, an envelope clutched in his hand, the Texas Monthly logo embossed in the corner.

"You ready for this?" he asked, his voice even, but there was something in his eyes—something charged, waiting.

Mae tilted her head, her heart kicking up a notch. "That depends. What exactly are we opening?"

Jim exhaled, running a hand through his hair. "The list came in."

She stilled. **The Texas Monthly BBQ Top 50 List.** The one that could change everything.

To most people outside the state, it was just a list in a magazine. But to anyone in the barbecue world—especially in Texas—it was *the* list. The gold standard. An inclusion could mean a line out the door for months. A Top 10 spot? That could change a restaurant's entire future. It meant national recognition. Food pilgrimages. Feature stories. Stability. Legacy.

The day Daniel Vaughn, the magazine's barbecue editor, had shown up, she hadn't anticipating being there. She'd just needed a break—from emails, deadlines, the blinking cursor that refused to cooperate. So she'd grabbed her laptop and drove to the only place that ever seemed to reset her brain: the porch at Rocket Ribs.

Jim was already out by the smoker, tending the fire with the quiet focus that always made Mae's heart stutter just a little. There was something about the way he moved—deliberate, unhurried, confident without being performative. She sat at the far edge of the porch, pretending to work, her fingers hovering over her keyboard as she stole glances over the rim of her mug.

When Daniel stepped through the doors of Rocket Ribs & BBQ unannounced—unassuming but focused, his sharp eyes assessed everything from the scent of the smoke to the bark on the brisket. He hadn't come alone—he brought a photographer, a notepad, and the weight of an opinion that could make or break a place like this.

Jim had kept his cool, guiding Daniel through the pits, explaining their process.

*"We don't rush anything here. Every cut of meat gets the time it needs to be perfect."*

She remembered watching as Daniel took his first bite of the brisket, his expression giving nothing away.

Then came the coffee. Jim had smiled as he placed a steaming cup in front of him.

*"You're not gonna find this at any other barbecue joint in Texas."*

Daniel had taken a sip, his brow lifting slightly. *"Smoked coffee, huh?"* Another sip. *"That's... something special."*

The rest of the visit had been a blur of questions and note-taking, and by the time Daniel left, there had been no clear indicator of where Rocket Ribs would land on the list—*if* it landed there at all.

Now, Mae stood beside Jim, staring at the envelope that held the answer.

"You want to do the honors?" Jim asked, holding it out to her.

Mae hesitated, then took it anxiously with a smile, the paper heavy in her hands. With a deep breath, she slid her finger under the seal and pulled out the letter. Her eyes scanned the page, her pulse hammering in her ears.

Then, she saw it. #7.

Rocket Ribs & BBQ had made the list. And not just made it—*they were in the top ten.*

Her breath caught. Jim's eyes darted to hers, disbelief and exhilaration warring in his expression. "Rocket Ribs & BBQ is number seven on the list."

Mae let out a stunned laugh, pressing her fingers to her lips. "Jim—"

He turned the page, skimming through the feature write-up. "Brisket, ribs, all the staples... but you know what set us apart?" He lifted his gaze to hers, a slow grin forming. "Rocket Smoked Coffee."

A rush of pride and warmth filled Mae completely. It had started as a challenge, a simple dare over a conversation that had changed everything. Now, it was part of something bigger—something that had shaped both their lives in ways they hadn't expected.

Jim exhaled, running a hand over his jaw, his fingers brushing against the faint stubble that had grown throughout the long day. "I don't even know what to say."

Mae did.

She stepped closer, slipping her arms around his waist, feeling the solid warmth of him as she pressed against his chest. His heartbeat was slow and sure, grounding her.

"Say you're proud of yourself," she murmured, tilting her head up to meet his gaze.

Jim chuckled softly, the corner of his mouth lifting in that familiar, boyish grin. "I'm proud of us."

The words settled between them, wrapping around her like the glow of the fire pit beside them. She smiled, her fingers tracing small circles on the fabric of his shirt.

The restaurant behind them was quiet now, the last few patrons lingering inside, but out here it was just the two of them beneath a sky slowly blooming with stars.

Mae leaned into him, her cheek resting against his chest. "You know," she said quietly, "I think I finally get it."

Jim's hand moved gently along her back. "Get what?"

She looked up, meeting his eyes, the firelight casting a warm hue across his face. "Why you came back. Why this place means so much."

His fingers found her waist. "And do you think you could love it too?"

Mae didn't hesitate. "I already do."

The honesty in her voice settled between them like a promise. Jim's expression softened, and he dipped his head, their foreheads brushing as he held her a little tighter.

"Good," he murmured. "Because I wasn't planning on letting you go."

Her heart swelled.

Jim dipped his head slightly, his gaze dropping to her lips. Slowly, he reached for her, fingertips brushing her cheek, then tangling softly in her hair. He leaned in, breath mingling with hers, their noses nearly touching—until he suddenly paused, his lips hovering a whisper away.

"I should probably warn you," he said, deadpan, "my kisses are low and slow... just like my brisket."

Mae let out a breathy laugh, grinning and rolling her eyes as she grabbed his shirt and pulled him even closer.

"Kiss me, you big hunk," she whispered, eyes shining.

And so he did.

At first, it was soft—a question more than a declaration. But then it deepened, full of heat and history and hope. Her hands slid up to his shoulders, anchoring herself there as the world around them faded. The past, the grief, the noise—it all fell away.

There was only this. Only him.

When they finally broke apart, Jim rested his forehead against hers, still catching his breath.

"I'm proud of us," he said again, softer now.

Mae smiled, fingers trailing along the back of his neck. "Me too."

And as the fire crackled and the night wrapped itself around them, Mae felt Sandy's words echo like a quiet benediction:

*Life is a story we get to write, chapter by chapter. There will be moments of heartbreak, moments of joy, and everything in between. What we choose to dwell on shapes the people we become...*

And as Mae looked into Jim's eyes, warm and steady and impossibly close, she knew—

This was home. This was the next chapter.

And this was just the beginning of their story.

# Thank You for Reading

If you've made it this far—thank you. I hope Mae and Jim's story brought you as much joy, comfort, and emotion as it brought me while writing it.

This is only the beginning of *A Texas Love Story*. Stay tuned—Book Two in the series—**There's Fire**—is coming soon, and with it, more heart, more hometown charm, and a few surprises along the way.

To explore upcoming titles, sign up for updates, or try some of that smoked coffee, visit:

**www.rocketribsandbbq.com/our-books**[1]

If this story meant something to you, I'd be honored if you left a review on **Amazon, Goodreads**, or wherever you purchased the book. Your words help others discover these stories and keep this small-town world growing.

From the bottom of my heart—thank you for reading.

Warmly,

**Rees Walther**

---

1.     https://www.rocketribsandbbq.com/our-books

# About the Author

REES WALTHER WRITES wholesome, emotionally rich romance stories rooted in family, community, and the redemptive power of second chances. Drawing inspiration from real-life moments of loss, healing, and unexpected joy, Rees crafts stories that linger long after the final page—stories where love feels earned and home is more than just a place.

Before turning to fiction, Rees spent 27 years serving in the Air National Guard and Reserves, including multiple tours in war zones around the world. He later retired from federal service at the U.S. Department of State. These experiences—marked by resilience, service, and a deep appreciation for human connection—influence the heart and depth found in every story he writes.

When not writing, Rees can often be found behind the smoker at Rocket Ribs & BBQ, perfecting slow-cooked flavors, roasting and smoking small-batch coffee, or sharing life's quiet magic with family and friends.